DENTED CANS

Heather Walsh

To Mike

One

October

This was the year it all went downhill.

Or maybe it had always been going downhill, and this was the year I finally noticed. It was hard to pinpoint the exact beginning of the slide.

It wasn't like we were some perfect Brady Bunch family before. God no. We'd always had our problems.

And now.

Now. We were like one of those wrench sets with the rows of sockets, and someone had come along and dumped everything out onto the floor and then tried to shove it all back without putting the pieces in their proper spots. But no matter how hard you tried, you couldn't close it unless things were put back where they belonged. It was impossible. That was us, everything jumbled up inside, threatening to spill out at any moment.

Maybe if we had known from the beginning, things might have turned out differently. Maybe there wouldn't have been seven thousand dented cans—or at least they would've all had labels. Maybe our house would have felt more like a home than a museum of all things Sampson. Or maybe I could've had a phone conversation without inhaling Lysol.

I looked over at Ben. Maybe he wouldn't have made all those noises. And maybe Ryan wouldn't have gotten that D. I guess trying to predict how it all might have turned out was pointless. Too late now.

But if I had known, I obviously would have treated them differently. We all would have. But how was I supposed to know? Why feel guilty about something you could not possibly know? Hindsight was 20/20 for a reason.

Should I have known, though? Maybe. Probably not. Sure, there were a few oddball things here and there that could have been clues. The scrapbooks maybe. Dad's dream of being on the Mr. Clean bottle. Or all zero-point-zero visitors at our house.

But nobody else noticed things growing out of control, that much was for sure. That responsibility—as usual—fell to me, and I admittedly had been too focused on getting out of North Prospect to notice or care. It was easy to look back now and see how bad things had become, but when you were just floating along down Screwed Up River, it was hard to cast your anchor and figure out where you were and how you got there. You didn't notice because things built up gradually, like a few spots of mold on a shower curtain, until all of a sudden you were washing your hair behind a slimy black sheet and you couldn't understand how it had gotten like this.

That about summed up this year.

Two

February

$3,777. That was how much I'd have after the deposit cleared. Mrs. Vercellone said she would need me to babysit again next weekend, so there was thirty more.

HONDA ACCORD Great Condition, 5 spd, air, 140K original miles, clean, new tires & timing belt, $3200. North Prospect.

I highlighted that one, although it sounded too good to be true at that price. I definitely wanted original miles—my ideal car would be one owned by an elderly couple who only drove it to church and Stop & Shop, the dual epicenters of North Prospect.

PONTIAC SUNBIRD exc condition, 140,000 miles, auto, ps, pb, $2300 OBO. Wetherstown.

Cheaper, but no way was I doing American-made, especially not as a used car. I might as well flush my money down the toilet.

TOYOTA COROLLA 5 spd, exc cond, 210K mi, Must See, 2 dr, $2100. Fairtown.

Very cheap, but way too many miles.

The first one had everything I wanted, but unfortunately it was out of my price range. I wanted to keep it under twenty-five hundred dollars so that I'd at least have something left over for repairs. Because if you bought a car for twenty-five hundred dollars, you were buying problems, guaranteed. And this car was going to have to be a workhorse. I needed four years of driving as far south as Virginia or as far north as New Hampshire. It was my escape pod. And you couldn't escape very far in a lemon.

My birthday was still months away, but I figured if I saw a really good deal I could just buy it and let it sit in the driveway. What did I care? As long as I ran the engine every now and then, it would be fine. I could even let Dad take it to work once a week. It would certainly be in safe hands, with the poster child for Allstate's good driver discount behind the wheel.

Ryan came into the kitchen.

"What are you looking at?" he said.

I highlighted another ad, even though I was finished. JEEP WRANGLER $13,995, CHERRY RED, 45,000 mi, 2 dr, 4X4, 6 cyl. Sure, why not? Let's throw in another cylinder or two. It was my fault for doing this at the kitchen table.

"Let me see which ones you highlighted," he said.

"I'm busy."

"So what, you've just moved from studying your school crap all the time to studying car ads instead? Won't your math books be jealous? 'Hannah, don't you love us anymore?'"

"And you've just moved from maybe getting a ride to the mall to never getting one."

"You're hilarious."

I looked down at the paper again, but I could tell Ryan the Hummingbird was putting together some sort of nectar concoction, like that peanut butter and sugar sauce he'd made last week. He had drowned his ice cream in it. Said he was trying to copy Friendly's recipe. Unbelievable. He should just inject glucose straight into his veins and save himself the trouble.

The sugar addiction ran strong in our family, though. I had it, too. Sometimes Ryan felt like a mirror on a bad hair day—he showed you what you looked like when you had absolutely no interest in such information. I knew I shouldn't eat so much sugar, but there were days when I just could not stop myself. But at least I tried not to make it so obvious. It was embarrassing to have an urge you couldn't control.

One time I was coming up from the basement, holding my stomach funny, and a whole bag of discount Halloween candy fell out from under my shirt, like I were giving birth to Mars Bars. I was mortified. Ryan saw it, and he didn't know whether to laugh or start raiding the floor.

I went to elementary school with this kid named Drew who was forbidden from having sugar because it made him too wild. That was how Drew himself put it: too wild. No cupcakes that people brought in for birthday celebrations, no churros y chocolate in Spanish class. Frankly, I couldn't do it. Diabetes, too. If I ever got diabetes, I knew how it would end: I'd cheat, sneak a Ring Ding, and then keel over because I couldn't stop myself. They'd have to lie in my obituary, since it would be too humiliating to go that way. Hannah Sampson, 38, Dies from Lack of Willpower.

But luckily we were all blessed with a furious metabolism to counteract the sugar addiction. In fact the Sampsons looked like a bunch of weak little sticks. Five praying mantises, the state insect of Connecticut. Or that poor beachgoer in the cartoon who was always getting sand kicked in his eye and his girlfriend stolen from him.

We were scrawny, but none of the Sampsons were hideous looking, at least. Mom, Dad, Ryan, and I were all decent-looking brunettes. Definitely not beautiful, but perhaps could legitimately be called cute. Then there was Ben. He was blonde and was currently hovering around extremely cute, with the potential to be out-and-out handsome one day. You would see kids like Ben only occasionally in town, those skinny blondes in the grocery line who older women couldn't help but make some doting comment about.

Ryan was preparing whatever it was very conspicuously to annoy me. It was working. Then Dad came inside and began brushing the snow off his jacket, also very conspicuously, to make me feel guilty. Even though I had already shoveled the driveway and sidewalks morning—for only ten dollars, which was criminal, really the need to go out there and push around the no missed. My dad, the consummate cleaner.

I was geared up to talk money with him after looking at those car ads. You had to be in the right mood to deal with his flawed logic. Not to mention his constant evasions of the subject.

I kept the highlighter in my hand so I would look slightly official. Some wire-rimmed glasses would have been nice, too. "Dad, you're going to try to help me pay for my college tuition, right?"

"You didn't shovel the left sidewalk completely."

"I did. What about college?"

"We'll do what we can."

"Well, I'm just trying to figure out a few things here. Approximately how much do you think you can help me with? Just a ballpark figure."

He didn't say anything.

"Five thousand a year? Ten?" I said.

"That's not fair. She gets ten thousand and I can't even get ten bucks allowance?" Ryan said. He looked up from his plate of saccharin.

"This isn't any of your business," I said.

"You might have to look closer to home," Dad said.

"I've told you before, there aren't any schools nearby that are good. And I'm not living at home," I said.

"Because it would be horrific if you had to do that, wouldn't it?" Dad said.

"I'd rather take out loans," I said, ignoring his attempt at a joke. "I'd go into massive debt before I'd go close to home."

"Yale's in Connecticut," Ryan said.

"I'm not going to Yale. And I'm surprised you even know that fact," I said.

"College is very expensive these days," Dad said.

"Can you please just give me an estimate on how you much you think you can help me out with?"

"I'm sorry your mother and I don't have higher-paying jobs, but we're trying our best."

"Why are you getting offended? I never said anything about our jobs."

"The answer is we'll try our best to help you out."

"Hey, I'm going outside," Ryan said, throwing his empty plate into the sink. "You want me to shovel anything?"

"Not without a hat you aren't," Dad said.

"I'm not wearing a hat. I hate hats," Ryan said.

"It's freezing out. Do you want to get sick? You lose eighty percent of your total body heat through your head."

"Fine, I'm not going then."

Dad left the room, and I looked back at the newspaper. I should've known he would do that. He had played his hand nicely, reversing the whole situation and trying to make me feel guilty. It was like a darn chess match with him. Suddenly out of nowhere his bishop flies across the board and blindsides you into check.

"He can afford it, I bet," Ryan said.

"Probably."

"Who are you kidding, he's going to give it to you."

"I'm not counting on it."

"They'd never give anything to me."

I turned the page.

"Anyway, he probably just wants you to go to UCONN so you can eventually set up a little desk next to him, and then you two can drool over numbers all day," he said.

"That will never happen."

"Or maybe he imagines how many dented cans he could buy with your tuition. 'Hannah, your books cost approximately seventeen hundred cans of wax beans.'"

I smiled. "He probably does."

"With your nerdy grades, you can get some scholarship, can't you?"

"I'm going to try."

He left, but I stayed at the table. I wrote down 2,500 and subtracted it from the total. 1,277. Plus thirty next week. That would barely cover two semesters worth of books and food. It was unfortunate that the car would just about wipe out my account, but what could you do? That car was my ticket out of North Prospect. So I needed to just plan on paying for the whole thing myself with loans and scholarships. It sounded like a failed Milton Bradley game. Loans and Scholarships. But I didn't have a choice. I knew I wasn't going to get showered with financial aid because we weren't dirt poor. And this way, if he did decide to help me out, it'd be a sudden windfall, an unexpected bonus. If not, then at least I wouldn't be disappointed.

Working at fifteen just wasn't worth it in the long run. The only option a fifteen-year-old had in this blue-collar town was bagging groceries at Stop & Shop. You could make more under the table babysitting than by bagging groceries. But once I turned sixteen, the day I turned sixteen, I would find a decent job and work as much as I could until I went off to college. I'd keep babysitting on the side, too. Every bit I saved now equaled fewer loans I'd have to take out later. Nobody else seemed to get that, but that wasn't my problem. I got it.

I knew I could sacrifice and wait. College would be worth giving up a few things in the here and now. Like Kyle Reid. He obviously liked me, and I could do worse. At least he wasn't part of the meathead contingency. But what was I going to do about it? You didn't just walk up to Kyle Reid and ask if he'd like to come over to your house and possibly stay for a nice meal—of peanut butter and jelly sandwiches. With your crazy parents who acted like the KGB had arrived at their house to spy on them when someone came over. So what if I had to wait until college before I had a real boyfriend? I could be patient. Unlike all these fools in my class, I didn't expect high school to be this incredible, mind-blowing experience. High school was like purgatory. You just had to wait it out until you got to the real deal.

I knew that I was inexperienced in all the ways adults complained teenagers weren't these days. I had never even smoked a cigarette, for God's sake. I'd tried a couple of swigs of vodka with Shelly and hated it. I'd been kissed exactly one time, and I was pretty sure it was the result of a dare. But how many high school romances ever amounted to anything? Besides, I wasn't the only sophomore in my class who had never had a real boyfriend. There were a handful of us in that little club. Sometimes people with boyfriends would try to include us by asking who we had a crush on, or who we liked better: Jock A or Meathead B. But I think once you were in the club long enough, people just assumed you would be in it until college and generally left you alone.

Even Shelly, who was in the club too for the record, didn't really seem to get how things worked. She claimed she was going to college, but she didn't understand that it was all a game, and if you weren't getting good grades, taking part in a few extracurricular activities, and scoring high on the SATs, then you weren't even playing. Unless of course you lived in Ridge Heights, the one small patch of wealth in town, or had a legacy admission spot—then you were exempt. Those were the rules. I didn't make them up. Well maybe they weren't hard and fast rules, but they were pretty close. There wasn't a ton of wiggle room if you wanted to escape North Prospect.

If Shelly had lived in Ridge Heights (the redundant name drove me nuts, by the way—how obsessed with towering over others could one get?), it would have been a given that she would be going to college. Most of the path would have just been laid out for her. Still, she was miles ahead of the pack. Look at my brother. Ryan had a perfectly fine brain, and was quite possibly as smart as me, yet he was headed straight for the remedial track at Wetherstown Community College, if he was lucky. You couldn't just make someone understand something like that, though. You couldn't just tell them and then expect them to suddenly start changing their ways.

But you'd think my brother would look around at the deadbeats in this town and try to avoid that fate. Did he really want to end up restocking the Roy Rogers condiment bar all day while counting down the minutes to his cigarette break? Or get sucked into that boredom vortex which begets cheap beer, which begets pot, which begets some form of opiate? And he was going to regret it someday. He was too smart not to. His eyes would open, the moment of enlightenment would come, and by then it would be too late. It really was unfortunate that you couldn't just strike the fear of the condimentist life into someone.

I went to my room to look through some past issues of the *Gazette*, our local paper. My mom read it religiously, although how she could do so was beyond me. It was the worst newspaper imaginable. The *Gazette*: serving Housatonic County, and its lack of news, for over seventy-five years. They always ran the most boring, insignificant stories on the front page. If there was ever a World War III, the *Gazette's* front page would read: Local Farmer Grows a Tomato, and in the upper corner in microscopic print it would say President Declares World War, See Page E7.

But it did have a great classified section. It was actually better than anything you could find online, especially if you were looking for an old, cheap car. The sort of people selling those still clung to their old-fashioned print paper. But the competition for anything in these classifieds was fierce—there were just too many Connecticuteers in need of cheap crap. When I did finally see my dream car, I would have to call right away before someone else snatched it.

"Hannah, pizza's here," Ryan said from downstairs.

"Pizza!" Ben said.

"Coming," I said.

Ah Sunday, the day of the pizza. And on the seventh day, the Lord rested and had himself a nice, hot slice of DeLuca Pizzeria's five-dollar large (offer only valid on Sundays, no toppings). Pizza was one of the few foods the Sampsons could all agree on. Ice cream was on the list too. And all but Ben liked our other treat, Chinese take-out, featuring those preternaturally red ribs. DeLuca's pizza was basically Ragu sauce splattered on thick, lumpy bread with some lukewarm, barely melted string cheese on top. But even bad pizza was still pizza, and ergo far superior to the majority of things we usually ate.

Ben started salivating when Dad opened the boxes, and he let forth a triumphant yelp when Dad put a slice in front of him. DeLuca's should hire him for their commercials.

Dad passed me a slice but avoided looking at me. He probably thought I was going to revive our tuition debate. Fortunately for him, I was never bringing it up again. I had conceded defeat. Checkmate.

"Hey Fuzzhead, you excited for pizza?" I said to Ben.

He made the sound of a bottle rocket flying through the air as his answer. But at least after making this sound he said yes. Sometimes you would only get one of Ben's noises as a response to your question. All of us were barely fazed by them at this point, but honestly I was probably the best at interpreting what he was trying to say.

"I need a knife and fork. Who else wants one?" Ryan said.

"Use the ones in there. They're clean," Mom said.

Ryan jerked the handle on the dishwasher. He was always so extreme with things. He had broken just about every item he had ever owned. No control. He was only fifteen months younger than me but it felt like triple that sometimes.

"Oh jeez," Ryan said. He turned toward Dad. "Why do you have to put our sponges and toothbrushes in the dishwasher? There's even a facecloth in here this time."

"It sterilizes them," Dad said.

"We are so weird. Nobody else in North Prospect has toothbrushes in their dishwasher," Ryan said.

"How do you know what other people have in their dishwashers?" Dad said.

Ryan sat back down and picked up his plate. "This is just not my day. Look at this thing. Why do I always get the pieces with no cheese and all crust?"

"It's karma," I said.

"What's that again?" Ryan said.

"Your fate. Destiny." He didn't need to know about the whole retribution part.

"Well, I need some new karma then," he said. "Hey, guess what this new kid in my class's last name is?"

"Spider," Ben said.

"No. It's Little. Alex Little. Can you believe it?"

"He can't help his last name," Mom said.

"Imagine how fun that guy's life is going to be. Little. He's pretty short, too," Ryan said. He looked down at his plate. "At least his first name isn't Dick."

"Ryan," Dad said.

"Or Stuart," I said.

"Yeah. He'd be doomed," Ryan said.

"We're not much better off. Crazy, long-haired man who gets backstabbed by a woman and kills thousands of people," I said.

"What are you talking about?" Ryan said.

"It's in the Bible. Go look it up."

"Forget it. It's not worth knowing that much."

We all then devoured our first couple of slices in minutes, because we all knew what cold DeLuca's pizza tasted like. When we had polished off the first pie, Dad wiped the corner of his mouth with his napkin and looked at us.

"Your mother and I have an announcement. We're planning a trip to Disney World."

"What? We've been there before. Who wants to go back there again?" Ryan said.

"Ryan," Mom said.

"What about the Grand Canyon? Or Yosemite?" Ryan said.

"I'd go to Yosemite," I said.

"Please, don't spoil this for your brother," Dad said.

"He probably doesn't even want to go, do you Ben?" Ryan said.

"Why would you do that? That's really uncalled for. Your mother is planning a nice vacation for all of you, you should be appreciative," Dad said quickly.

Clever of him, to keep rambling on like that so Ben couldn't answer.

"When are we going?" I said.

"Probably in the beginning of October," Dad said. He looked at Mom.

"Yes, that's right," she said.

"What?" I said. "I can't do that, that's during school. Why

aren't we going in the summer? Or during one of our school breaks?"

"Because it's cheaper, I bet," Ryan said.

"Hannah, you can miss five days of school. Besides, it's the least crowded then," Dad said.

"You know, you can ride donkeys down into the Grand Canyon," Ryan said.

"That's during my junior year, the worst possible time to miss school," I said. "You know what, why don't I just stay home? I'm old enough to be here by myself."

"Hannah, that's enough. You're the oldest, so you're supposed to be setting the example," Dad said.

"I'm the oldest, which is why I don't want to go to a playground for small children," I said.

"Nobody in this house cares about what I want," Ryan said.

"Ben's too young to remember the last time we went," Mom said.

"It was only two years ago," Ryan said.

"It was four years ago," Dad said.

Ben wouldn't remember it this time, either. I was surprised Ryan hadn't pointed that out. If I had thought the trip would actually matter to Ben, then of course I'd be behind it. But the truth was Ben wouldn't care where we went, Ryan would just whine the whole time, and I would ignore everyone. As usual I was the only one who could see when something was not going to go well, and yet I knew no one would listen to me if I told them this. I should have been named Cassandra.

"At least we go on vacation. You're very lucky. How many other families get to go to Disney World more than once?" Dad said.

"A lot in my class. But not that many have gone to the Grand Canyon," Ryan said.

"If I have to miss school, then I'd rather it be for Yosemite," I said.

"Yes, let's just all go to separate places for a family vacation," Dad said. "We'll spread out across the country."

Whenever he said some wise guy comment like this in front of Mom, he never looked over at her. I think he was embarrassed for not being able to remain serious all time the way she could. You would never catch her making a comment like that, and certainly never catch her laughing at one of ours.

"Sounds like a great plan to me," Ryan said.

"We're all going to Disney World, and that's that," Dad said.

"Fine," Ryan said. "You want to go, Ben?"

"Fine," Ben said, copying his tone exactly.

For the record, I did not verbally consent.

Ryan popped the rest of his crust into his mouth. "So where's Easter this year?"

"Where do you think it is?" I said.

"Nonnie's," Mom said.

"I know, let's have it here instead of at Nonnie's. We have it there every year," Ryan said.

"We're going to Nonnie's," Dad said.

"But we never have a party here. I bet it's because Aunt Lydia won't go anywhere else. She gets special treatment just because of Cousin Eddie. When was the last time you saw him, anyway?" Ryan said.

They didn't answer him.

"It's a valid question," I said.

"Eat your pizza," Dad said.

After dinner I went back to my room. That was the saving grace of this house, that we all had our own rooms. What would do if I had to share? Good Lord, I'd go crazy. I sat down on the bed and began to work on my *Great Gatsby* essay, which struck me as ironic after my Ragu and string cheese dinner. You could be sure Gatsby, Old Sport, didn't wash and reuse sandwich baggies. Here was a guy who understood how to take control of his life. All that karma/destiny talk was actually total nonsense. Gatsby knew what he wanted and went after it, no questions asked. He didn't look back, didn't worry about anyone else. He just plowed ahead.

Frankly, my family really wasn't my problem. I didn't choose to have children. It was harsh, but it was the truth. Gatsby knew it. It was hard enough to look out for yourself in life—you were lucky if you could even manage that. Ryan wasn't a child, although he did act like one. And of course I worried about Ben. You wouldn't be human if you didn't. He was my baby brother after all (baby being the operative word there), and about as innocent a person as you could find.

But at least they had me to pave the way, while I didn't have anything remotely useful to guide me. I had to figure it all out on my own. If Ryan didn't want to follow my example and ended up as a Lettuce and Pickle major at Wetherstown Community College, what could I do about it? Nothing. And what could I really do about Ben?

So what was the point of worrying about things you couldn't change?

Three

April

Whoever came up with the idea of school pictures should be shot.

When Mr. Mathews handed me my package, I didn't even have to open it to see how awful the picture had turned out. Thanks to the big cellophane window showcasing a blown-up version of my face, anyone within a hundred feet could see that for themselves. My chipped tooth was glaringly obvious, to start with. The photographer must have zoomed in on it somehow. Nobody else's picture looked this zoomed in. I should say none of the other three people in the entire school who ordered pictures. Who ordered pictures in high school, anyway? Wasn't that supposed to stop in the fifth grade? Thanks to Mom, we still did every year. There was no way getting out of it, either, because she knew when they were taking them: same day as Ben's school, where she worked. Still, the photographer could have at least managed to get me smiling. They probably had the janitor from another school take them to save a couple bucks. Who else could have gotten that unprofessional shot of me? My lips half-parted and my head tilted back. It looked like someone had been aiming a leaf blower directly at my face. Thanks, Janitor Bob.

When I heard Ben and Mom come home, I brought Mom the pictures. As soon as she spied the top of the package, she held out her hand.

"Let me have them, please."

Even though she said let me have them please, it was more like she growled give me those things, now! No one could stand in the way of her and her obsession with photography.

She sat down at the table and started flipping through the package to ensure that all seven million unnecessary copies she had ordered were accounted for. Janitor Bob did not disappoint there. I was trying not to be rude by leaving immediately, but she seemed to have nothing to say about my delightful photo, so I looked down at her hand instead. I think everyone in the family was downright shocked at just how good of a job Dad the Rock Collector had done with buying her engagement ring. Probably even Mom. Frankly, I'd have a tough time coming up with another thing he'd ever done that well. It had a large, brilliant diamond, which of course did not hurt. But it went from being your standard pretty ring to an extraordinary one because of the emeralds surrounding the diamond. It was like the green of someone's eye, hypnotizing you when you looked at it straight on. You never saw a ring like that on the fingers of any woman in North Prospect. Knowing Dad, he probably gave the jeweler a hard time, too. Or he could have even made it himself. Sue, I've selected, polished, and cut these gems for you. Emeralds are a semi-precious stone. They have a hardness of six and are found in the following countries: Brazil, Kenya, and Sri Lanka. Oh, and will you marry me?

She was still sorting through the horrible pictures.

"I don't like the way—"

"Hannah, get me a scissors please."

I got them from the drawer and gave them to her. They were our only good pair, the ones with orange handles. The rest were all terrible. They were the type you were handed in first grade, along with paste. They couldn't cut through Jello.

She started following along the white borders of the pictures, depositing tiny squares of me all over the table. I couldn't look away from that chipped tooth of mine. I probably could have used braces. But I was borderline. It wasn't like people jumped back and yelled whoa, what's going on in there when I opened my mouth. Even if they did, I'd still have to jimmy the money out of Dad's wallet to pay for them. Just not worth it. At least I didn't have a vampire fang like Bryan Ackerman. That might have kept me in the No Boyfriend Club well into college.

"What do you plan on doing with all of these?" I said.

"The big one goes to Nonnie, we'll put these in the scrapbook, this goes to Grandma Lyons, these to Aunt Nell and Aunt Lydia."

"Why does Aunt Lydia, or Aunt Nell for that matter, want a picture of me? This picture is terrible anyway."

"Where are Ryan's?"

"I don't know. I don't keep tabs on him."

I went upstairs to do my homework, and did not leave my room until Mom called us for dinner. When I was sitting down at the table, Dad turned from the counter.

"Any guesses what this is? Nineteen cents for it." He held up a silver can that looked like it was hobbling along on a crutch.

"Why do you buy those things? It's so embarrassing," Ryan said.

"He just told you why he bought it. Because it was nineteen cents," I said.

"That's a huge markdown. Do you know how much cans normally go for? Besides, there's nothing wrong with it. You could drop this from a three-story window and it'd still be fine," Dad said.

"Yeah but it might be beets or something nasty that nobody will eat," Ryan said.

"It could be dog food," I said.

"It's not dog food," Dad said. But he did have a bit of a twinkle in his eye as he said this, as if he was daring it to be dog food just to see our reactions.

"Let's find out what we've got here," he said.

He took the can opener off the counter and fit the two round pieces that looked like tiny circular saws onto the can. He squeezed the handles together and then turned the crank, and the saws began to tear through the metal. It was easy going for about two seconds until they reached the crushed part. The can opener stopped in protest. Dad leaned forward and closed his mouth, as intensely focused as a bullfighter, as if one wrong move would spell disaster. He reversed the crank and then jerked it forward again, and the little circles rode down the metal hill and up again. They squeaked around the rest of the can, as if they were cheering about finally returning to undented, unmarked-down metal.

"It's peaches!" Dad said.

You'd think he won the lotto.

"What a surprise," I said.

"They look great, we'll have them for dessert," Dad said.

Of course it was peaches. It was always peaches, the kind with those little strings that would inevitably get stuck in your teeth. The peach shelf stocker must have been one clumsy guy. Honestly, Ryan and I probably wouldn't have minded eating them, because there was enough sugar in one can to power a small village. But even we didn't eat the peaches. It would only encourage him, and suddenly he'd be bringing home seventy dented cans a week instead of ten. I wouldn't be surprised if he roamed the aisles and "accidentally" hit specific cans with his elbow so they'd end up on the dented shelf next week. Oh look, Progresso chicken noodle. How'd that get in there? Amazing. Only fifty-nine cents!

"When did you start buying dented cans?" Ryan said.

"What?" Dad said, jumping a bit as if he'd been startled. "I don't know."

"Did you buy them when we were little kids?"

"I think so."

"What about before we were born? When it was just you two?"

"What does it matter?"

"Did he sweep you off your feet with a can of Bartlett pears?" Ryan said to Mom.

I chuckled. And they ignored him.

"Hey Dad and Hannah, you want to do my algebra homework

for me? You can race to see who's the smartest," Ryan said.

"No," we both said.

"Dad, do you have to do algebra at work?" Ryan said.

I knew why Ryan constantly tried to keep the conversation going. Because unlike me—who had no problem sitting there and staring at an empty peach can, marking time until dinner was over—he had no tolerance for silence or boredom. So impatient with the world. If I was able to wait out high school, what was yet another uneventful Sampson dinner? My strategy was passive resistance, and he'd be wise to employ it himself once in a while.

"Not very often," Dad said.

"What does an accountant do all day? Just add up numbers?" Ryan said.

"Dad cooks the books," I said.

"What does that mean?" Ryan said.

"He defrauds the U.S. government," I said.

"No he doesn't. If he did, he'd be getting some cash out of the deal. Obviously he isn't." Ryan tapped the can of peaches.

"Good point," I said.

"All right, that's enough. When you two have a career, we can all discuss our responsibilities," Dad said.

Truth was, Dad had a pretty good job for someone in North Prospect. Being an accountant did technically make him white-collar, but when you lived in a blue-collar town, acted like a cheapskate, and never pushed your kids the way Ridge Heights parents did, it didn't much matter what your job was.

When we finished eating, Dad brought a bowl over to the table and put the can of peaches in front of him. He began to spear the orange bulbs with a fork and drop them into the bowl. Of course he purposely did this in front of us so we'd all be reminded of which prize he'd won. He held the bowl toward Ryan, who shook his head. Ben made a loud noise, something like brreeeeenng-brreeeeennng, the sound a phone might make if it were being stabbed, when Dad passed the bowl near him. You couldn't take that personally though, since Ben's palate consisted of about seven items total. Dented peaches weren't on the list. I held up my hand before Dad even offered them to me.

"If nobody wants any, then your mother and I will enjoy them by ourselves," Dad said.

I turned to Mom.

"You got *Dr. No*, right? Are we watching it tonight?" I said.

She nodded. "After the dishes are done."

Then she stood up and began doing something that I had always found bizarre. She took a pitcher from the dishwasher and then went over to the bottom cabinet where we kept the cake mixes and potato chips and brought out a white box that was about as tall as Ben. She lugged the box over to the counter and used a measuring cup to scoop the powder from the box into the pitcher, creating white dust clouds that floated to the ceiling each time she emptied the cup. She filled the pitcher with water, stirred it with a wooden spoon, screwed the top back on, shook it twice, and put it in the fridge.

My mother had just made milk.

None of us kids would go near the stuff, so she was still forced to buy normal milk. Only she and Dad drank it. They claimed they preferred the taste, but it was obvious that what they preferred was the price. Delicious, milky savings.

Mom told me to start the movie and she'd join me in a bit. We had already watched *Dr. No* a couple of times together, but I didn't mind. I liked this little ritual of ours, and frankly I loved old James Bond movies. He was too much, with his license to kill and his revolving door of girlfriends. The outrageousness of it all was hilarious to me, the way Bond was metaphorically talking about sex every two seconds. I mean, *Octopussy*? How did they ever get that title through? I was embarrassed just to say it in front of Mom. I couldn't understand how she could sit there stone-faced the whole time. I always laughed my entire way through them.

Two females watching James Bond movies—it was pretty funny if you thought about it. Mom and I never did much in the way of mother/daughter activities, and even with movie night you'd think we would watch *Terms of Endearment* or some mushfest like that, but no. 007. I think being surrounded by so many boys had contaminated us.

I started the movie, and Mom came in a bit later. Halfway through it, I turned to her.

"They need Jaws in this movie. He was so much better than this pathetic villain."

"Jaws comes back in *Moonraker*."

"Oh, right."

Her mind was like a steel trap when it came to anything Bond. You could not stump her. I had decided a few years back, when I actually took some time to think about the matter, that Mom might be fairly intelligent. I think I'd put it at about a 50% chance of being true. Which would mean that filing permanent records for minimal wage all day must have been pretty mind-numbing for her.

My own memory was decent. I didn't have a true photographic memory, but at times I could close my eyes and conjure up an image of the past. The license plate on Dad's old Nissan as it sat under the carport: MRD 119. The strange part was, I could remember really specific scenes like that but then forget whole chunks of my life. And I would have never known that I couldn't remember them if it hadn't been for Mom's obsession with cataloguing every breath we took. I would flip through the scrapbook and clearly remember when our pool got built by the red-headed guy who never seemed to run out of plaid shirts. I could even hear the sandpaper in his voice. But then I'd turn the page and find a set of twenty pictures of us at a fair that I supposedly went to around the same time but had no memory of at all. And later in that same book I couldn't for the life of me remember Ben's birthday party, even though there I was, looking very determined to be bored. Memory was a funny thing. And I couldn't even ask Mom about any of it. Whenever she caught any of us looking through a scrapbook, she'd tell us to put it away. Which made no sense. Why slave over all of these books if you were never going to let us look at them?

\#

I spent most of Easter mass thinking about how I still did not believe any of this. That was what Easter and Christmas had become for me—a bi-annual confirmation of my non-beliefs. I had stopped believing most of this stuff years ago, at least the Catholic bit. I just didn't see the difference in believing in Jesus and the Virgin Mary and believing in Zeus and Aphrodite. I wasn't about to take a stand on the existence of God, though. My answer to that one was a big I didn't know. The atheists seemed just as obnoxious to me as the organized-religion people.

It was clear that Mom didn't believe any of this, either. I could just tell by looking at her. I wasn't so sure about Dad, since he did seem to recite the prayers with genuine feeling. He was the best Catholic in the family, hands down.

During the homily, I started imagining what it would be like when I had my car and driver's license. How I would be able to say, you know what, I'll meet you all at church. What freedom! I could listen to my own music, loudly, instead of Ryan's ramblings or Mom's complaints of a headache. Just imagining *that* was exhilarating—driving to college seemed almost unfathomable.

When I was done daydreaming, I began to thumb through the missalette, looking for interesting names and Greek phrases. I found an actual picture in there, of Jesus raising his arms to the Heavens and emitting beams of light, so I held the place with my finger and handed the book to poor Ben, for whom I imagined this hour must have seemed like ten, although he would never fuss. I thought the picture might remind him of his favorite cartoon character, He-Man. He smiled at it. And then Ryan saw that I had given Ben some attention, so he started whispering in his ear and got Ben to giggle for the last ten minutes of the mass.

"Ryan, can you please explain to me why you can't sit still for fifty minutes?" Dad said when we were in the car afterward.

"No."

"We asked you to leave your younger brother alone," Mom said.

"Can we please stop talking about this? I was just whispering a few jokes to him so he wouldn't be bored."

"Do you think your mother wants to spend her time at church policing you?" Dad said.

"Yeah, who'd want to miss that homily? That was the most incoherent one to date. If I handed that in as an essay to Mr. Marak, I'd fail. There was no point to it whatsoever," I said.

"Maybe he should hire a speech writer with our donations," Ryan said.

"It would help," I said.

"Let's leave Father alone please," Dad said.

It would be useless (but frankly satisfying) to point out that neither he nor Mom listened to Father the other fifty Sundays of the year. We went to church on Easter and Christmas, that was it. He's killed, then He's born at the end of the year. We show up for both.

It was rare for me to deviate from my usual strategy of passive resistance and actually try to help Ryan out, but I did feel slightly at fault for showing Ben the picture. And there was Ben just looking out the window during all of this, with no concept of homilies or Saviors.

I turned around.

"Hey Ben, let's play What's Next," I said.

"Yeah," Ben said.

"I'll play," Ryan said.

"I don't know if we've discussed this matter—" Dad said.

"Dad, you play too," Ryan said.

"I have to concentrate on driving," Dad said.

I waited until we came up to a bend in the road.

"OK, what's next?" I said.

"McDonald's," Ben said.

We turned the corner and passed the Golden Arches.

"You got it." I always tried to give him something easy, like a landmark.

"What's next?" Ben said.

"Dark blue house, brown shutters, Virgin Mary statue with Christmas lights around it in the front yard," I said.

"And a basketball hoop that's missing a net," Ryan said.

We all turned and looked out the window.

"There it is," I said as Ben smacked the glass. "OK. What's . . .next?"

"White house."

I was trying to give him the high school, but he was smart to guess white house. There were only about ten on every block to choose from.

Ryan laughed. "You got it. OK, my turn."

"What's next?" Ben said.

"In about ten seconds there will be a creek with a few sickly trees around it and an old air conditioner on the bank," Ryan said.

"And a pair of faded sneakers tied to a branch," I said.

"There!" Ben said when we passed it.

"OK good job," I said, taking out my book.

"What are you reading?" Ryan said.

I held the cover toward him but kept on reading.

"*Night?*" he said.

"It's about the Holocaust."

"That's depressing."

I ignored him.

It was funny how Ryan and I did look like "What's Next" prodigies. But the drive to Nonnie's was just another thing I'd been able to memorize. If someone moved a brick on one of the buildings, I could probably call them on it. But it was almost cheating. I mean, how much brainpower did it require when every house in town looked basically the same? Long and squat, like a shoebox. Like those dioramas they had us make in elementary school, where you'd take a box and then glue a page from a magazine on the inside of it for your background. And it was always something completely inappropriate, like an ad for gold watches from the JC Penny catalogue. Then you'd find a few figures to live in your diorama, like your brother's armless G.I. Joe, and glue them in so they were stuck forever doing the same thing. A perfect little diorama family. What was the point of those, anyway? To teach you how to glue? Or maybe it was to brainwash you into staying in North Prospect forever? Lesson not learned for me—that stale glue had worn off on my feet, thank you very much.

"Hey Hannah. You know what I like? I like how Jesus gets to have his name capitalized all the time, even if it's just He said or He walked. God too. I wish I could get that deal," Ryan said.

"Can't you ever just be quiet with your own thoughts?" I said.

He looked over my shoulder and started to read out loud to get back at me, but I pushed him into his seat.

Honestly, he was right about *Night*. It was depressing. And I was still under the spell of the last book I'd read, *The Adventures of Huckleberry Finn*. I definitely wasn't ready to leave that world. I could see myself in a straw hat with a kind of relaxed smile, standing over a raft, my mouth casually working on a piece of grass. Huck was escaping his small town, too, his problematic family. And sure, in this fantasy world, I could grab Ben and take him on the raft with me. The two of us could float down the river, free from it all, dipping our feet into the cool water and looking up at the beautiful moon.

As soon as we walked through Nonnie's front door, a sense of lethargy overtook me. No matter what, we always ended up here for any family get-together. Then again, we didn't have much of a choice. Mom was an only child, and everybody on her side was dead. Well, except for Grandma Lyons, but I think you could put five strangers in front of her and tell her it was the Sampsons and she'd barely know the difference. We only visited her at the convalescent home once a year, and that was enough. But Nonnie's was barely a step above a convalescent home. There was nothing to do, which inevitably made Ryan antsy, which meant he would bother me. We had looked everywhere and had not been able to find a single game in the entire house, not even checkers or Old Maid. Was it really such a shock, with Dad being able to entertain himself for hours with a hunk of shale? But you'd think there would have at least been an old deck of cards lying around, for God's sake.

We received the usual awkward hugs from everyone, and then, just like every time, Ryan and I said we were going to take Ben outside. Even I knew that staying indoors meant being bombarded by my aunts' annoying questions. There were only so many times you could answer how's school going. And if I tried to hide in a corner to read, they would cluck their tongues and mumble about how rude I was, which would only activate Mom and Dad to come guilt me into talking to people. So outside I went. Nonnie's yard may have been the size of my little toe, but it was still better than extra Aunt Lydia exposure. And just like every time, our cousin Steve followed us, even though he had to know by now that Ryan and I couldn't stand him. Zero games in a house would do that to you.

Ben ran ahead of us and immediately began stomping on the ground. And it went without saying that he made a noise as he brought his foot down. It sounded like a pair of giant handheld cymbals crashing.

"Got him!" he said.

"I think I see one there," I said.

He stomped. Then the cymbals. "Got him."

Poor Ben. Mom and Dad would never admit there was anything wrong with him, but it just couldn't be normal behavior for an eight-year-old. Although I did know for a fact that he never actually stepped on the bugs. He stepped next to them. I would be the only one in the family to notice a detail like this. And frankly it made Ben even more sweet and innocent in my eyes, if that was possible.

"There's another one over here," I said.

He came over to me, and I pointed at a fat ant about ten feet away. I did have pretty good eyesight.

"I see him," he said.

I tapped the back of his hair. "Go get him, Fuzzy Wuzzy."

He shook his head at me as he walked away. No combs for Ben. His hair was actually getting pretty long, which meant Mom would have to drag him to the barber soon, offering him a new toy as a bribe. It was as if Ben had a secret bowl cut, like invisible ink or glow-in-the-dark stickers. You could only see it when you untangled it with a comb dipped in conditioner, which happened about once a year. If you looked at him straight on, you would see nothing out of the ordinary. But if he turned just an inch, and you caught a glimpse of the back of his head, you would encounter crazy land. A mop of fluff and knots that formed this great blonde fuzzball. It was at its most impressive in the morning, and then it would gradually become more and more deflated, as if the knots had spent the day working themselves out. But he would just have to go to sleep and then sure enough, he'd wake up with the fuzzball back again in all its glory. Like Father said. All glory and honor is yours, almighty Fuzzball, now and forever. Amen. Getting his hair cut did help—maybe that was why he hated going. Maybe Ben realized that he was special because he was the only blonde in the family, so he wanted to keep as much of that hair as he could. Some people might have a hard time proving if they were ever blonde as a kid, but not Me and My Scrapbook. Boring brown hair always.

Steve was holding a gun that shot foam arrows, and he started waving it in our faces when he realized we weren't paying attention to him. That kid had a brand spanking new toy every time we saw him. Aunt Nell had probably decided to buy it for him this morning with the sole purpose of making my brothers jealous.

"Hey, let Ben try that gun out," I said. I was trying to fix Nonnie's lopsided bird feeder, although I don't know why. It hadn't seen any birdseed inside of it since the Nixon years.

"No way, he'll break it," Steve said.

"Steve, I bet you can't climb that tree," Ryan said.

"I bet I could."

"How about you don't try," I said.

"Here, I'll hold your gun while you climb it," Ryan said.

"No, I don't think so," Steve said.

He shot one of the arrows, and everyone except for me ran

after it. Ryan reached it first and lifted it high in the air.

"Let me see the gun," Ryan said.

"No, give me my arrow back," Steve said. He came over and tried to grab it from him.

"Just let Ben try it for a second."

"No. Give it to me. You go buy your own gun."

Ryan handed him the arrow. "So what if you have a dumb toy? Our Dad secretly told us that your mom couldn't get anyone to date her. So Nonnie and Grandpa paid your dad to do it."

"Shut up. That's not true," Steve said.

"Sparks," I said. This was my nickname for him. I told him once he was like a spark plug, always igniting the fires. I used it when he amused rather than annoyed me—so obviously I used it very sparingly.

"Then why don't your parents ever kiss in public?" Ryan said.

"Well at least I don't wear Payless shoes," Steve said.

"And at least I'm not some bought husband's bratty kid," Ryan said.

Steve started running toward the house.

"Oh no you don't, you little tattletale," Ryan said, running after him.

"Now you've done it." I turned to Ben. "Come on. Run with me."

"OK," Ben said.

He did a pitch-perfect imitation of a motorcycle as he ran. He even twisted his hand around an imaginary handlebar as if he were revving the engine. As soon as we got inside, Steve ran up to his mom. He ran right into her, actually. Ryan came up behind me.

"Mom—" Steve said.

"Hi Aunt Nell," Ryan said.

"He said that Uncle John said that you couldn't find anybody to marry you so they had to buy Daddy and that makes me a child brat," Steve said.

"And he called my clothes and sneakers Goodwill and made

fun of Ben and said we're poor kids in pov—" Ryan said.

"I did not!" Steve said.

Now, I probably should have been watching Aunt Nell and Uncle Ian the whole time, to witness their reaction, but I wasn't. I was looking behind them at Dad, who was sitting at the table. And when Steve said the bought Daddy thing, my dad's face went red exactly at that moment. It was remarkable.

Then Aunt Lydia, who was wearing a pleated skirt that looked like one of those paper cupcake holders, moved closer to Steve and put her hand on his shoulder. She started brushing at his shirt, as if she were trying to remove the Sampson Disease we'd put there. And she was glaring at me. At least we were spared from Uncle Reginald coming over to join in the fun. Steve's hair could have been on fire and he still wouldn't have turned away from his football game.

"Hannah, where were you in all of this? You should have been supervising them. You're the oldest," Aunt Lydia said.

"You think I can control them?" I said.

"Don't talk back to your aunt," Dad said.

You would have thought he had said your aunt is my most favorite person in the world and has also just been declared the winner of the Publisher's Clearing House with that smug look plastered all over her face. And who in the heck wore a skirt like that? Who woke up and said, today is the day for the cupcake skirt. Besides, what she was really saying was not that I was the oldest but rather the *girl,* and in her warped 1950's view that meant you were a slave to biology. Your job, first and foremost, was to mother. So many women in North Prospect were like her—if anyone gave off even a whiff of a challenge to their backward ways, they became defensive. Everything I did seemed like a rejection of these women's choices: wearing pants instead of skirts, speaking my mind (to men especially), planning on going to college and not some secretarial school for two years until I got married and ended up barefoot and pregnant in the kitchen.

Aunt Lydia was a hypocrite to boot. She was obsessed with her church duties, like arranging the flowers on the altar every week or planning the coffee hour after mass. So holier-than-thou. She must have been trying to get in good with God because she produced a delinquent son, had a spaced-out husband she never talked to, and treated her relatives like dirt. Sorry, but I didn't think putting a bouquet of mums on the altar erased all sins.

We tried to go back outside, but Mom followed us and said we were eating soon. So we watched TV—the tiny, ancient TV in the backroom that Uncle Reginald wasn't hogging—for a while. Another banner holiday. We didn't even have an Easter egg hunt. Ben would have liked that. It was as if they refused to admit there were actually kids here. A few minutes later, I went into the kitchen to get a drink, and I was treated to seeing millions of Hannahs scattered all over yet another kitchen table. There was my leaf-blower face framed for all the world to see. There were even more pictures of Steve with his arm around baby Elisabet, who looked like she was about to scream bloody murder. Ben's and Ryan's school pictures were there, too.

"Oh here, Sue. Did you get this one? This is just Elisabet," Aunt Nell said.

"Thanks," Mom said.

"Here Lydia, these are yours," Aunt Nell said. She handed her a stack of about a hundred pictures.

It was clear that I was surrounded by crazy aunts. I had one who thought she was dressing for the bakery display window, and another who thought she was the Goddess of all Mothers, even though she had only produced two measly kids. And one of them was named Elisabet, for God's sake. What sort of name was that? Did she want her to have to spell her name to people until she was 80? Aunt Nell was the sort of mother who acted as if she were the only person in the whole world who had figured out how to procreate. Ever since precious Steve had first graced the world with his presence, she had made him take all these stupid Sears pictures in the most ridiculous poses: here's little Stevie wearing a fireman's hat, here's Steve sitting on a sled indoors with some confetti snow. In June. And then she'd hand them out like we were in the breadline just dying for them. Aunt Nell was the complete opposite of Mom. They both took a million pictures of their kids, but Mom glued them down and shut them up in books.

Except for my school picture. That was the only one she ever gave out. Just my luck. Maybe it was because she hadn't taken it. Or maybe she wanted to show Aunt Nell up with her three, count 'em, three children.

Dinner was announced, and I parked myself in my usual place next to Ben and Ryan at the end of the table. Unfortunately, Steve and Elisabet were down there too. But who was complaining? I'd rather sit in the trenches of Babyland than down next to Uncle Reginald or the June Cleavers.

Aunt Nell kept spooning food onto Nonnie's plate while Nonnie just sat there and watched it all pile up. I started wondering if I hadn't missed out on an opportunity by never talking to Nonnie. None of us kids did. We would always just escape outside as soon as we arrived, eat some food, and then go back outside or watch TV. Then give her a limp hug and go home. She probably had a few entertaining stories in her, about the war or what Dad was like as a kid.

But then again, Nonnie never talked to me much, either. Her only granddaughter. Well Elisabet did count, technically. Fine, her only granddaughter (who could feed herself). No one talked to any of the Sampson kids. The only people around the table who I had ever had a real conversation with were my parents and my brothers. And barely even them. Their silence was certainly fine with me—preferable even—but odd nonetheless.

I kept letting all the food I had no interest in go past me, but the potatoes, probably the only thing I actually liked, were still stuck down by Uncle Reginald.

"Uncle Reginald, can you please pass the potatoes?" I said.

Everyone else called him Uncle Reg. Not me. It was Uncle Reginald in my book. Why waste a name like that? I don't think he even noticed anyway. I could probably call him Uncle Moronic Fool and he would just nod and look past me.

Mom emerged from the kitchen with Ben's plate of chicken

nuggets and put it in front of him, and he immediately made a little cheering sound. Before she sat down, she took a few exciting pictures of everyone eating, because we definitely didn't have enough of those choice shots. I was surprised Nonnie's dining room table hadn't gone blind from all the times it had seen a flash go off in its face.

After a few minutes of precious silence, Aunt Nell looked at Aunt Lydia.

"Did you see what was in the *Gazette* the other day? Who wants to march in Wetherstown?"

"Who?" Aunt Lydia said.

"The KKK. Can you believe it? Isn't that awful?" Aunt Nell said.

"I know, I read that too," Uncle Ian said, nodding. He was the type who would sit there just waiting for an opportunity to show you he knew more about something than you did. "Some people are trying to stop them from marching."

"Well, I don't think that's right. I'm not racist of course. I certainly don't agree with their views, but it doesn't seem fair to not let them march. Everyone's entitled to," Aunt Lydia said.

"Everyone in Wetherstown is a bunch of fools," Uncle Reginald said.

"Oh! Did I tell you that Steve joined Little League?" Aunt Nell said.

Oh, here we go.

"Good. Every boy should play baseball," Uncle Reginald said.

"That's right, Reg. That's what I told her," Uncle Ian said.

Mom and Dad said nothing, probably because they didn't know how to properly interact with adults since we never had any visitors and they didn't have any friends.

Ryan looked at me for a second and then slowly closed his eyes, which actually made me want to say something for once. I could point out that neither he nor Ben had ever played baseball, and they still turned out fine, or that Cousin Eddie probably did and look what happened to him. Or I could make a joke and we could all laugh around this table for once, something like hey, did you know my dad's the star hitter for his accountant softball team? Except they don't use a real ball. They just roll dice to see what base you go to. But as usual, I let reason and logic prevail, along with a generous dose of self-restraint. There was no point in saying anything—no one would listen to me or acknowledge if I made a valid point. I would have to just keep honing my passive resistance skills instead.

They kept going on and on about how great baseball was for building a boy's character and teaching him life lessons, whatever that meant, and then something very strange happened. I caught Aunt Lydia staring at Ben, and I could have sworn she was about to cry. She didn't seem to notice that I was watching her. In fact, she didn't seem to notice anyone or anything but Ben. She just kept looking at him with this terribly sad expression. Up until now, the only emotions I'd ever seen on that face were anger or annoyance. She seemed like a different person at that moment. Unrecognizable. Then, just as suddenly as it began, the expression cleared and she looked over at Dad, making some snore of a comment about her bathroom sink.

I was sure it had to do with Cousin Eddie. While they all sat around talking about what kind of glove Uncle Ian had bought Steve, there was this scandalous family story practically dangling in front of us, just flapping in the wind. Funny how easily families migrated to the mundane.

\#

When we finally left, I waited until Dad had driven for a few minutes before I said anything.

"Hey, how old is Cousin Eddie? Twenty-five? Thirty?"

Nobody answered me.

"Schizophrenia runs in families, you know," I said.

"Don't worry about him," Dad said.

"I can't believe I have a relative that I've never met. I could pass him on the street and never even know that I'm walking past family," Ryan said.

"You pass through a mental institution often?" I said.

"Hannah," Mom said.

"You don't know that he's in one. Is he? Or is he on the streets? Which one is it?" Ryan said.

"Nobody knows. Don't concern yourself with it," Dad said.

My interest in Cousin Eddie was barely registering a simmer so I wasn't going to push it— although if there was a mental illness involved I wouldn't have minded knowing for the genetic information. But it was ridiculous that all they ever did was ignore the questions or pass around the same stale rumors. You would think I was some stranger and not their own flesh and blood with the way they acted. I could never get anything out of them, especially anything about the past. It was as if they expected me to believe the world started the day I was born.

I looked out the window, and we passed by a police car with its lights on. The blue light reminded me of my favorite rock in Dad's collection, the pale blue one that looked exactly like a cascading waterfall of toothpaste.

You had to wonder what would make a person start collecting rocks, of all things. Did he just stumble across an interesting one on the ground one day and then it took off from there? From what I could tell, Dad did have a pretty impressive collection. He even had some fossils. When I was younger I used to walk around with my head down, always on the lookout for unusual rocks. If I found a one, I'd bring it home to him and he'd put on his jeweler's monocle and tell me how it was formed, what made it special. We hadn't done anything like that in years.

His most valuable piece by far was the amethyst geode in the corner of his rock room. It was remarkable, how something so gray and commonplace on the outside held such a treasure inside: thousands of deep purple crystals, with white ones that looked like spun sugar bordering the hole. Mom had bought him that geode as a wedding present. I can't remember how long it took to get that juicy piece of information out of her. She probably felt guilty about getting such a stunner of a ring while he got nothing.

We all went to a rock show a few years ago, and the whole time Dad kept drooling over this one piece made out of a stone called malachite. It was different shades of green with these intricate swirls in it, like a maze that would take days to solve. Dad must have gone back and inspected that rock a dozen times. John, just go ahead and buy it. But Sue. I don't need it. It's not the wisest use of money. And on they went. He paid a couple hundred dollars for it. From then on, I knew he was slightly crazy. Why do all this work to save thirty cents on a can of split pea soup and then blow two hundred bucks on a rock? Even still, I'm glad he did. That malachite one turned out to be my second-favorite piece.

"Dad, can you leave me the blue toothpaste rock in your will? And the malachite and amethyst ones?" I said.

"Don't talk like that," Mom said.

"You can have the whole collection," Dad said, sweeping his hand across the windshield. He was trying to look magnanimous, but the truth was he knew I was the only one in the family who wouldn't sell them off for a profit or use them as a doorstop.

"Did you bring the leftover stew home?" Dad said to Mom.

"Yes," she said.

"Why? Who wants to eat that stew two days in a row? Once is more than enough," Ryan said.

"Here's a fun game: Let's all keep quiet and look out the window," Dad said.

Four

June

I had finally found my car. As soon as I saw the ad, I knew. This Civic was speaking to me. I just about threw down the *Gazette* and ran to find Dad the moment I saw the magic number: $2,500. I had waited long enough. As the eldest Sampson I knew how it worked around here: pick your battles very selectively and then plow on through.

Besides, it wasn't like I was asking to go to some guy's house for a co-ed group sleepover, the way the cool people in my class did. They were lucky to have repressed little me, president of the No Boyfriend Club. I was asking to buy a car with my own hard-earned money! They didn't know how good they had it, or what sort of teenager they could be dealing with. Ryan might show them one day though, and when he did, my Civic and I would be long gone.

I knew I had to approach Dad about the car. Mom never made any major decisions. If a conversation you were having with her got too heated, she would pinch the bridge of her nose to signal her impending migraine and you knew what was coming next: go ask your dad. And even if you somehow got her to side with you, you couldn't use it as collateral with Dad. He would null and void it because you had bothered her in the first place, and now you had a distracted, cranky person to try to reason with. But just to complicate things further, you had to wait until they were both together, because if you didn't he would deflect by saying he had to get her in on the conversation.

Luckily they were both outside—Dad was skimming the pool and Mom was vacuuming it. What a team. Someday I would have to find a husband who pitched in with all the chores like Dad did.

I showed him the ad, and I could tell that he had immediately dismissed it. It could have said Free Mercedes and he wouldn't have given it the time of day.

"I just think it's too soon to run off and buy one," Dad said, handing the paper back to me.

"I'm not running off," I said. "You don't know how long it's taken me to find the perfect car. I can't keep arguing, I've got to call them."

"I don't see why there's such a rush," Dad said.

"It's the law. I didn't decide that sixteen is the age when people can legally drive."

"That doesn't mean you have to own one the day you turn sixteen."

"No. But it means I can."

"Your birthday is still months away."

"A car is so expensive. Do you really need this?" Mom said.

"I know how much it costs, trust me. I'll have enough remaining to cover anything that can go wrong."

"You can't know what will go wrong. A new engine or transmission would be well out of your league," Dad said.

"And there are a lot of crazy drivers out there," Mom said.

"Why do you have to act like the apocalypse is coming? It's pessimism twenty-four-seven around here," I said.

"I didn't realize a faulty transmission was part of doomsday," Dad said.

"Dad, why—" I said.

"Don't yell, please. My head," Mom said.

"I'm not yelling," I said, talking more slowly. "I've saved a long time for this. I've read the ads in the *Gazette* religiously. I've checked online. This is a good deal for a sturdy car."

"You could save the money and use one of our cars. It's a lot of money for someone your age," Dad said.

"Are you going to let me buy the car or not?"

I had to let them see that I was going to be just as stubborn as they were. I hadn't babysat for countless hours and cut their spotty lawn strewn with sticks that would jump up and bite me in the legs for nothing. This car was my escape from North Prospect. It transformed my college search radius. I would not budge on this.

"Let us think about it a little more," Dad said.

I stormed off without answering and went into my room. All of a sudden Ryan came in.

"They're being dumb," he said.

"You heard?" I said.

"Yeah. I was in the back by the shed."

"Why are they acting like this is a complete surprise to them? I've only been talking about buying a car since I was ten."

"My brain is very confused. It's going into overload because for once it wasn't me getting yelled at."

"I knew he'd try to pull something like this."

"Just buy it, Hannah. They won't stop you."

"I have to call that lady right now or else it will be gone. There's a good chance it already is."

"You do that. I myself am going to watch some TV because there's nothing to do in this house."

And then I did something I really never had done. I defied my parents. Normally I just relied on my passive resistance to get by, able to go along with everything they said by convincing myself that I could wait out their ridiculousness until college. But now I called the number, and when an elderly woman answered I realized this really could be my lucky day and this car just might be as good as it sounded. Truth was I knew how to pull out all the stops when I needed to. I could be even be charming—or at least I knew what adults wanted to hear. I made sure my voice lost all of its sarcasm or edge: "I'm a high school student who is looking for a car for college and I think the Civic you are selling would be perfect for me. I'm even using my own money that I earned through babysitting to pay for it. Could I come see it?"

It worked. She promised she would not sell it to anyone before I had a chance to look at it.

And then I went back outside and calmly told my father that I had called the woman and scheduled us to look at it on Saturday.

He looked at me and said nothing. I wasn't exactly afraid, but I was nervous. Who wouldn't be? It wasn't easy to have your father staring at you like that, trying to decide if he is going to let you be an adult, or at least adultlike, or if he's simply going to tighten the reigns even more. And unfortunately Mom had gone inside, which left the door open for more deflecting.

"OK, we'll go and take it to a local garage and see what they say," he said finally.

Part of me wanted to squeal. Unleash my inner teenage girl. Or maybe even hug him. But instead I just said OK, thanks Dad, as if that was exactly what I had expected him to say.

I thought about nothing else that week. Saturday, a day that was typically uneventful for me (but this would change in college!), was something I finally got to look forward to the way all the kids with keg parties to attend did.

The fact that we were going to be dealing with an elderly woman was a relief to me. If it were another man around Dad's age, we'd be in trouble. Whenever he was around a male peer, he would become so submissive. His voice would grow louder, unnaturally friendly. He was like one of those dogs that would lie down as soon as any other dog approached and just wait obediently to be acted upon. It drove me nuts.

But elderly women loved him. When they looked at him you could just tell what they were thinking: what a polite young man! It's so good to see one these days. He reminds me of my son.

Miraculously, it all went smoothly. Dad and I took it for a little test drive to the garage, and the mechanic said there were no major problems with it. And the price was so good that even cheapo Dad didn't think we needed to negotiate. I had put in so much effort to get to this point that as I sat in the passenger seat of a car I was about to buy with my own money, I could not enjoy the moment. Instead I kept waiting for something terrible to crop up. Like the brakes failing. Or the lady's obnoxious children charging in to put an end to their mother's senile transaction. But she just smiled and told me to take good care of it when I handed her the check, and Dad arranged to pick it up after work on Monday with Mom.

And he did! My car, my very own car, was sitting in the driveway, waiting for me to get my license.

This car emboldened me. I felt like Gatsby even more—"don't look back" was my motto. Now I needed my family even less. Instead of having this abstract dream of college to cling to, I had a machine that I could actually reach out and touch. I had my escape pod.

And so newly emboldened, I embarked on my next project: finding something to do. With summer here, I realized there was only so much college prep, babysitting, web surfing, and car washing/ogling that I could do to fill the hours of the day. Yes I needed to study for the SATs and get my newly depleted savings account back up, but I was a teenager after all. I needed some fun. And I wasn't going to find any here.

Our backyard was small—it barely even fit the pool. Maybe I could have kept myself busy in a big backyard with some woods to explore or a creek to curl up next to with a book, listening to the sound of the water as my background music. You couldn't tell where our postage stamp of a yard officially ended and the neighbors' began, since there weren't any shrubs or a fence marking the border. You simply had to draw imaginary lines between the houses for the sides and look at where the Bakers decided to stop cutting their own little patch of lawn for the back boundary. There weren't any people my age who lived nearby, and all of our neighbors basically kept to themselves. We never saw the old people to the right of us except when they took out their trash. And to the left was a forty-something-year-old weirdo who still lived with his parents. Excitement Central around here.

So the day after my car was securely in the driveway, I decided I had to have Shelly come over. I had a respectable number of casual friends, but Shelly was the only one I ever really saw outside of school. Having her come to my house was the only answer. The whole situation had become extremely embarrassing. So far, I'd been over her house dozens of times, and she'd been over zero-point-zero. The excuses I had been coming up with lately were ridiculous: Ben has a cold and he's contagious. My dad is working at home today, so we aren't allowed to watch TV. The carpets are being cleaned. I was tired of lying and I was out of excuses. Frankly, I had been for weeks. But no more! So what if my house was cluttered, or if my parents hated when anyone outside the family was there and made their discomfort very obvious. I was ready for it. Besides, people in the No Boyfriend Club needed to hold tight to whatever friends they had.

The bell rang, and I marched right up to her and asked if she wanted to come over after school. And she said yes.

We met up after last period and took my bus home together. For the first time since elementary school, I actually had someone to sit with. As soon as she walked through the front door, she started looking around. She probably thought I had been keeping some secret from her the whole time, and now she was trying to figure it out. But the kitchen was actually one of the more normal looking rooms in the house.

We went into the living room. While we were watching TV, I looked around and tried to imagine what I would think if I were seeing this room for the first time. It was pretty incredible, the amount of stuff we had been able to cram in here—there were piles of something or other just about everywhere you looked. Nothing like the sparse, functional living room at Shelly's house. But what was so odd about this room was that even though it was brimming with stuff, everything was excessively clean. Dad made sure of that. For instance, right under the TV there were tons of CDs and books, but they were neatly stacked. And constantly dusted. They'd definitely pass the white glove test. But you got the feeling that they would fall over if you went within ten feet of them. This whole house was like that. Lots of clutter that looked all neat and orderly but in reality was about to topple over, like we kept trying to stack one more ace on our already wobbly house of cards. One day Dad's dust cloth was just going to knock the whole thing over.

"I'm thirsty. You want some water?" Shelly said.

"No thanks. The glasses are above the sink."

She went into the kitchen, and I started to flip through the channels. After a couple of minutes had passed, I got up to see what was taking her so long.

"Hannah," she said from the kitchen.

I stopped. "What?"

"Why are there locks on the cabinets under the sink?"

Oh boy. I'd forgotten about those.

She came into the living room and looked at me with her head tilted sideways.

"For my brother," I said.

"Ben?"

"Yeah."

"But he's like eight."

"I know. My parents are little weird about that kind of stuff."

"What are they scared he's going to guzzle some Drano?"

"I guess. He wouldn't though. Weird, right?"

"Yeah it is."

"I know, look at all these CDs and books," I said, waving my hand dismissively as if I were an outside observer like her and not a card-carrying member of this household. "Could we possibly have any more?"

"I saw them. Hannah, I love this place. Why didn't we come here sooner? There are all these cool, weird things to discover."

"Oh yeah? How about this. That locked cabinet under the sink."

"Uh-huh?"

"Only my dad has the key to it."

"Crazy."

"Did you look in the fridge?"

"No."

"Go look."

She went into the kitchen.

"Holy crap! How did they fit so much stuff in there?" She came back into the room looking like she had just seen a real live dinosaur walking around the kitchen.

Right then I decided I was just going to go ahead and do it. Go for broke. It was the power of the car willing me to take a chance. It was my Dad not flinching when I told him I had phoned the elderly woman. And so newly emboldened Hannah figured, what the heck. Just make a joke out of it and see how it played out. And if I didn't show her, who would I show? I had to allow at least one person into my crazy cocoon, since it obviously wasn't going to be a boyfriend.

"You think that's nuts? Want to see something even crazier?"

"Yes."

"I'm not kidding. It makes this look like nothing."

"Show me now."

"OK. Follow me."

I took her down to the basement and turned on the light.

"Whoa." She stood there staring.

"Hold on, that's not even it."

But the basement certainly was a good warm-up for the main event. The room was a complete fire hazard, another contradiction in the land of Mr. Safety. There were scrapbooks jammed into bookshelves, crates of Ryan's old video games in their original boxes piled high, jackets that didn't fit us anymore bursting out of the closet, our juvenile artwork hanging on the walls. We must've looked slightly disturbed to her: the family that never threw a single thing away. I couldn't remember it ever being this bad. It was as if our museum's permanent collection just kept growing.

I let her stare a little while longer.

"Come here. This is where it is." I took her into the next room, which we called the pantry, although I think Dad just started calling it that one day to make a room he spent so much time in sound fancy. It was wall-to-wall cans in there. Shelves heaving under the weight, bearing every size and color imaginable. If a food had ever made it to canned form, it was in this room somewhere. Because it was physically impossible for five stomachs to keep up with the onslaught of weekly purchases, many of the cans looked old and haggard. A fine layer of dust fell over all but the newest of cans, because even an obsessive like Dad couldn't keep this place clean.

I turned to see her reaction.

"Oh my God," she said.

"I told you."

"Who would ever use all these cans? There must be thousands of them."

"Ryan and I tried to count them once. We gave up when we got to three hundred."

"There are like ten Snow's Clam Chowders here. No, make that twenty. It keeps going back further."

"I know. Crazy, right? It's like they're planning for a nuclear war."

"And they're organized." She sounded impressed.

"That's my dad. Well, Mom too. They both help put them away. Soups are here, vegetables there. These are miscellaneous cans, like gravy or Spaghetti O's. Here's the fruit. And check out this section." She followed me to the corner.

"Who took all the labels off?" she said.

"They come like that. Have you noticed anything different about most of the cans down here? Take a look at this guy." I reached over to the fruit section and handed her a can of sliced pineapple.

"They have prices on them, in marker."

"Yes, that's right. What else?"

"The barcode thingy is crossed out."

"Very good. But there's one more thing. Look carefully, sometimes it's hard to notice."

She inspected a couple more cans before answering.

"They're dented."

"That's right. Dented cans are marked down, which is why my dad likes them. Even if there's only a tiny dent, they still knock off like half the price. But these fellas here in the corner are special. They're dented *and* unlabeled, so you don't know what's inside. They're even cheaper."

"It's like a mystery surprise!"

"Like a grab bag."

Shelly laughed. "Hannah, I love this. It's so freakish, like some kind of OCD thing. I can't believe we've been going to my house the whole time."

"You want me to heat you up a can of clam chowder?"

"Nah, let's go watch TV."

#

The next day was the last day of school, and everyone, even the teachers, was in a good mood. During English class, Shelly handed me a piece of paper. She had drawn a picture of a dented can and had written "What treat awaits?" across the top of the page. As I looked down at that can, I really felt like a fool for not having her over sooner. But I wasn't the only one in the family who had ever been a little embarrassed. Ryan once told me how he'd washed off the top of a can before he opened it at his friend Jake's house, and Jake couldn't understand why he did it. Ryan said he felt like telling him if you saw our pantry you'd know why, but instead he just made up some excuse. But that was just it. You didn't realize that you had all these idiosyncrasies because they were just hiding quietly in the dark, like a comfortable mole in its tunnel. Then all of a sudden somebody came along and shined a light on them, and you were left feeling awful, crouching in your tunnel, blinking at that sharp light. If everyone in your house did something, if everyone washed off the dusty, three-year-old can from the pantry, then you just assumed the rest of the world was doing it.

But I didn't care anymore if my family was slightly nuts. Let them be. Soon enough I'd be out on my own anyway (don't look back). Besides, our town was full of families that looked normal when you saw them in church or at the bank, but I suspected that if you peered into their windows, what you'd see would be far from normal. Everyone was screwed up, it was just how good you were at faking it. The families related to me sure seemed to prove me right. Now I could be proud of my freakish pantry, or of my uncomfortable mother who jumped about five feet into the air when she saw Shelly sitting on our couch. Proud that I wasn't going to fake it anymore. I was going to embrace reality.

But my good mood didn't last very long. Life would be better if the bad days just started out that way. Otherwise it was such a tease. Even the thought of my car didn't help—it was as if the fact that I now owned it had already been cemented in my mind, and so thinking about it was no different than thinking about a pair of jeans I owned. Its power had vanished, just like that, after one bad day.

During gym I hadn't felt like changing into my gym clothes—I figured Mr. Dobson would just give us a free period on our last day. But instead we played Steal the Bacon, a game where two teams lined up facing each other and players took turns racing a person on the opposite team. When Mr. Dobson called your number, you and your opponent were supposed to sprint toward the middle and try to grab the bowling pin (why it was called the bacon, I have no idea) and make it back without getting tagged. Now I was fast. And I could be very competitive, especially when I was around other competitive people, and especially if it was something I was good at. Mr. Dobson was a conservative old man nearing retirement—although he was still in surprisingly good shape—and I was sure he gave me the same number as a guy on purpose because he hated seeing a girl run out there so quickly and grab the bacon. Any time I was up against another girl, I could practically stroll back to my team before she could catch me. Especially if it was one of the fat girls. Or fat boys, even. Although I did always feel bad for the fat kids when we played and never ran very fast when I was paired against one, because you could just see that they were already miserable enough as it was. I'd always suspected Mr. Dobson was a closet misogynist. He resented me for stealing the most bacon and earning the most points. He and Aunt Lydia should get together to complain about this new generation of bold, assertive girls.

My shirt had ripped really loudly as soon as I took off, and at least half of my team had laughed at me. And it had ripped right near my ribs, so my blazingly white stomach flashed out at everyone. It was my fault for sprinting like an idiot when I realized stupid Andy Hansen had the same number as me. He stole the bacon, and I ripped my shirt. And I couldn't even get a new outfit out of the deal, not with Mom the Amazing Sewer on hand. I could rip the thing half a dozen times and she'd still be able to sew it up perfectly. And when it was finally time to toss it, you get oh no Hannah, don't throw that out. We can use it for something. I can make curtains out of it. Or let's at least put it in a mothball-filled box and store it in our permanent collection. I know, let's never throw anything away. Let's just save it all!

But the clincher came after last period, when they brought us back to our homerooms to hand out report cards. I got a B in English, my best subject. And the thing was, I knew that grade was wrong. I absolutely knew it. I had been keeping a solid A/A- all year, and the final exam—which was one long, purely subjective essay—counted 20%. But I would have had to have gotten a D on it to get a B, and I knew I hadn't. I had never gotten below a B- on any essay in my life! As angry as I was, I didn't even bother fighting it, because I knew this particular teacher would never in a million years admit that he had made a mistake. And I knew my parents weren't the Ridge Heights type to storm in and demand a recount for their child—they would just tell me to accept my lot as they had in life. I felt powerless yet again.

Still, I did sometimes feel like patting myself on the back on report card day. I had gotten all A's and one false B even though I grew up in an environment of cultural illiteracy. People talked about the price of gas or baseball gloves, not Shakespeare or even the politics of the day. For God's sake, I learned about *A Christmas Carol* through a Disney movie, where Scrooge was a duck and Bob Cratchit was Mickey Mouse. There was our very own dad on TV, the poor accountant getting swindled by his boss, having no drive or ambition. Boy, was Mom angry at us that day. Ryan and I had Ben in hysterics, making all these comparisons to Dad and ad-libbing dialogue: oh please Mr. Scrooge, my poor son Tiny Ben needs a new He-Man figure, can't you give me that raise you promised? Please, our family's roof is hanging on by a few pieces of duct tape. It's starting to leak. I doubt Ben understood the comparison, but the idea of his father as Mickey Mouse was probably funny enough. Ryan and I could have kept it up all day, we were so on fire, but Mom came in and figured out what we were up to. She got so mad that she turned off the movie and hid it from us as punishment. It wasn't until years later that I learned it was actually a novel by Charles Dickens and that Scrooge ended up giving Cratchit the mother lode of all presents at the end. Maybe there was hope for Dad.

That afternoon, Mom came home with a bag of corn on the cob, and she asked me and Ben to shuck it for her. I liked doing repetitive tasks sometimes as long as it was only occasionally—I could never file permanent records like she did day in and day out. And I was actually craving something mindless after my bad day. Plus, spending time with Ben always took my mind off bigger issues. We brought the corn outside along with two buckets, a small one for the husks and another for the corn.

I started to shuck an ear.

"Shuck some corn, Ben. Shuck," I said.

"Yeah, shuck corn," he said.

Shuck was one of those words that felt great to pronounce. Shuck. That and jalopy. Shuck some corn next to Dad's jalopy.

"Like me, watch," I said.

I grasped a piece of the husk and yanked it downwards, unveiling the yellow and white kernels.

"Partly shucked," I said.

I brushed at the kernels a few times to rid them of the silk, but it wouldn't come off. So then I tried picking the strands off one at a time, but that was ridiculously inefficient. It really started to frustrate me—I was practically clenching my teeth, all over some corn silk. Not exactly the mindless distraction I was looking for. I finally gave up and began to peel off another section of the husk.

"OK, you try," I said.

He tore at the husk, taking as much as he could fit in his little hand, and pulled the section right off. He made the noise of a handsaw cutting through metal, a sharp, piercing sound, like zeeyaah.

"Wow, you did half in one pull. Let me try that." I yanked a big handful all at once and made the zeeyaah noise.

Ben laughed.

"Nooooo, that's not right," he said. He ripped off the other half and did a much better version of the noise than I had done.

"All right, I'll just say shuck then. But let's see if you can get that string stuff off, smarty pants."

"Mom can!" He dropped the cob, covered with silk, into the bucket.

"Ha! Yeah, Mom can." I ripped the last piece of husk off mine and dropped it in there next to his.

We worked through the corn, with Ben saying zeeyaah and me saying shuck, shuck, like a couple of complete goofballs. I was actually starting to enjoy myself, shucking corn with him in the sun. I felt relaxed, and my bad day and powerlessness seemed distant. Ben was just about the only person who was incapable of annoying me. Shelly could get on my nerves sometimes with the way she'd rattle on about boys, as if she or I were going to do anything about it other than talk, talk, talk. Everyone else in my family annoyed me hourly. I wouldn't even wish for a world full of Bens, though. Because you needed the annoying people to remind you how special someone like Ben really was.

We finished pretty quickly since we only took off the husks and not the silk. I had Ben carry the lighter bucket inside, and I brought in the one with the corn.

I handed Mom my bucket. "Here you go."

"What's this? These aren't finished. They're full—"

"Sorry. It was hard to get that silk off."

Ben had put the bucket on his head and was now standing perfectly still and holding it there with his hand, like one of those villagers in Africa. I grabbed the bucket off his head and ran toward the trash.

"Hey." He said it really fast and short, as if he were being timed, and then caught up to me. We threw away the husks, and then I went to put my hand on his head to lead him into the living room, but he ducked under it just in time to avoid my touch.

I left him in front of the TV and went upstairs to my room. I realized I'd forgotten to tell Shelly about ripping my shirt in gym. She would love that story—and now I was finally in a good enough mood to do the story justice. Part of the reason I got along with her so well was that she tended to laugh at even my lamest attempts at humor. She was the sort of person who made you feel funnier than you knew you really were.

When I picked up the phone, I almost choked. It smelled toxic, as if he had sprayed approximately seventeen cans of Lysol on it. I held the thing as far away from my face as I could, and then I slowly brought it closer and smelled the earpiece. He had sprayed it there, too!

Obviously, my father had gone off the deep end. I could never get a boyfriend living in this crazy house, even if I'd wanted one. He'd try to kiss my ear and suddenly stop because it smelled like a sanitarium. Of course this also meant my father had snuck into my room when I wasn't there to perform his germ dousing. I hated the idea of anyone coming into my room. It was a violation. This was the one place I had to myself in this house. What father snuck into his fifteen-year-old daughter's room to disinfect a phone? That bothered me more than the Lysol. I think sometimes they all forgot I was female, just because I didn't behave like a little teenybopper. I had been so wrong to think having a quirky family was cool. Who would be proud of this?

I slammed down the phone. This one definitely did not belong in the passive resistance column. As soon as we sat down for dinner, I turned to him.

"Dad, why the hell did you come into my room to spray Lysol on the earpiece of my phone?"

"Hannah, the cursing," Mom said.

"I thought the mouthpiece is where the so-called germs are," I said.

"Phones are magnets for germs," Dad said.

"Not the earpiece! My hair smells like Lysol now," I said.

"Look at it this way. At least it'll kill the lice," Ryan said.

"I believe Lysol technically would kill lice," Dad said, half-smiling.

"OK, this is the complete opposite of normal," I said.

"Don't be so dramatic," Dad said.

"And you sprayed like an entire can on my phone. Why don't we just pipe Lysol through the vents? Flood the whole house with it," I said. At least that would keep him out of my room.

"I didn't spray the earpiece," Dad said.

"Well thanks for your restraint."

"You'll thank me when you don't get sick."

"Dad, I don't care if you spray the doorknobs or the light bulbs or whatever the heck it is that you spray. But at least promise me that you'll stay out of my room."

"Hey, this has strings all over it," Ryan said, taking a strand of silk off of his corn. You'd think he was at a fancy restaurant pulling some stranger's hair out of his soup.

"You can thank your sister for that," Mom said.

"You're welcome. And don't forget Ben. It was a team effort," I said. Then I took an exaggerated bite of my corn, strings and all.

I certainly wasn't trying to get Ben in trouble. In fact that was an impossibility. I was just pointing out that he was their favorite. It wasn't news to anyone here. We all knew they devoted all their attention and energy to him. It didn't bother me, though. It was Ben, after all—if anyone deserved to be spoiled, it was him. And it must have been hard for him, with Ryan and me fifteen months apart, and then along comes Ben six years later. Still, I'd always thought it was a little odd that Mom and Dad just out and out chose him as the favorite. No questions asked, no appeals, case closed.

I suddenly remembered I was still losing the phone fight. Dad hadn't promised anything.

"Answer this question, Dad. What good do all your clean doorknobs and phones do, anyway? Ben still gets those ear infections. We still get colds," I said.

"You would get sick more often. Trust me on that," Dad said.

"That's not even true. You don't want to kill all bacteria or viruses or you end up with the superviruses. We need some bacteria, like the kind that live in our stomach and are waiting for this fine pot pie to reach them," I said.

Ben laughed.

I did realize that I was lecturing more than usual because it was Report Card Day.

"We watched a video in biology where they filmed a person's eyelashes and skin magnified hundreds of times. You cannot even imagine what's there," I said.

"Hannah, please. We're eating," Mom said.

"I want to know. What's there?" Ryan said.

"Not while we're eating," Mom said.

"But I'll have to learn it one day. I'm just getting a head start," Ryan said.

"Oh, calm down. It's not a big deal. There are millions of microbes living there, like mites and bacteria, feeding on your dead skin cells. We actually watched them eating. They're everywhere, you just can't see them," I said.

Ben looked duly impressed. I had a feeling this topic would be right up his alley.

"They're not on your earpiece," Ryan said.

"That's why you need Lysol," Dad said.

"It's like that tapeworm in a jar that Mr. Dillon has in his classroom. It's so long and nasty—" Ryan said.

"Eeeww," Ben said.

"Ryan," Mom said.

"Imagine having that thing in your stomach. That's why people say 'he has a tapeworm' if someone eats a lot but doesn't get fat," Ryan said.

"I have a tapeworm," Ben said. He took a bite of his chicken nugget.

"That's enough of this talk," Dad said.

My impromptu microbe lesson was a nice prologue to my report card unveiling. I drew it from my back pocket and handed it to Dad. Ryan shot me a look of anger which quickly turned into misery, but I simply shrugged as if to say, I didn't invent the system, my friend.

"Where's yours, Ryan?" Mom said.

"Upstairs."

"Go get it," Dad said.

"I'll get it after dinner."

"Now," Dad said. He looked mine over and gave me his usual good job, Hannah, and then Mom did the same. But as they were looking at it, they seemed to regard it as some sort of code they had been unable to decipher, and were just saying good job because they guessed that was the appropriate response. They were better at handling Ryan's inevitably lackluster results.

He came back downstairs and thrust it toward Mom.

"You got a D in Spanish," she said.

"A D?" Dad said.

Wetherstown Community College, welcome your latest recruit.

Mom passed it to Dad.

"Ryan, your grades have never been this bad," Dad said.

"Lo siento, but that teacher sucks. Everyone in my class got a bad grade. The highest was like a C. So that makes mine really a B," Ryan said.

"Your mother doesn't feel well. And now you go and bring home a poor report card. And your final report card, at that," Dad said.

"Maybe it's because I'm a year younger than everyone else in my class?"

Dad just shook his head at him, but even I might be willing to admit it was possibly a factor. His birthday was at the end of November, later than anyone else's in his grade.

And I did understand Ryan's outlook on academics, even though I didn't agree with it. In the Disney *Christmas Carol* household, where you had no reference for schoolwork, you probably didn't see the point in trying very hard. If Ryan studied something that interested him, for example ancient Egypt, he would ace it. Of course I could have been a role model for him, but he refused to follow my lead. His loss.

"You've never gotten a D before," Dad said.

"Let me have a look at this," I said.

"No, it's none of your business." He tried to grab his report card from Dad. "Look, it's too freaking hard to learn a language in high school. We all sound like a bunch of dopes when we talk. We talk Spanglish. They should teach it to us when we're four, not fourteen."

"He's actually right," I said.

"I know I am," Ryan said, clearly surprised that he was.

"We have windows of time when it's easiest for us to learn things. For languages the window is when we're very young," I said. OK, even I was growing tired of hearing myself talk. But I felt like I had to purge that B somehow.

"See?" Ryan said.

Dad raised his hand, pointing his index finger at the ceiling. He always did that right before he delivered a lecture. It was a nice little warning system, like a tree that curled up its leaves before a big downpour.

"You are forgetting that you don't have a choice. In an ideal world, yes, it's probably better to learn a foreign language when you're young. But you have to take Spanish now, and you have to pass it." He shook his head. "You've never gotten a D."

"The only good day I ever had in that class was when we got to eat churros y chocolate. Everything else is so boring. Memorizing the names of farm animals or knowing when to use por or para. Who really cares?"

"You're not watching TV or playing video games for two weeks," Mom said.

"No me importa," Ryan said.

"He doesn't care," I said.

"Thank you, O Genius. Let me see this thing." He took my report card off the table. "What's the matter, Hannah? You're slipping. Look at this B."

"Yeah, well that B would look like the shining star if it were on your report card," I said.

He gave Ben a watch this look, and then looked back down at the report card.

"'Hannah is the biggest ass-kisser I've ever met. She's a pleasure to have in class because she scrubs my windows and cleans my erasers. Sometimes she teaches the class for me, even when I don't want her to.'"

Ben laughed, although I think it was because Ryan said in it a funny voice.

"What did your mother tell you kids about that language?" Dad said.

"Beware the green-eyed monster," I said.

"I'm not jealous of you. You're a nerd," Ryan said.

"A nerd who got an A in Spanish," I said.

"I know Spanish," Ben said.

"Let me hear it," I said.

"Dee os my-oh," Ben said.

"What does that mean?" I said.

"Ohmygod," Ben said.

Ryan and I grinned, and Dad made a face that resembled a smile, although it could have been indigestion. But of course Mom looked serious. She hardly ever smiled, or grinned, or smirked. Actually, that wasn't completely true. Once in a while I'd catch her smiling during a James Bond movie. Never during real life, then.

"Maybe you should go upstairs and start reviewing your Spanish book for next year," Dad said.

"No gracias," Ryan said.

"You're getting a nice vacation and this is how you act?"

"I don't really want to go to Disney World," Ryan said.

"I'd like to suggest that *I* skip out on Disney World, actually," I said. "So I can keep getting good grades."

"You're both going," Dad said.

"It's really going to affect my schoolwork," I said.

"I don't want either of you to bring it up again. You're both going," Dad said.

After dinner I locked myself in my room and sat on my bed. I looked down at that erroneous B on my report card, and I started to feel helpless again. I had no control over having an unfair grade staining my permanent record, and no control over spending my vacation in infantile Disney World. Or choosing to live in good ol' North Prospect. I was stuck in a boring blue-collar suburb where the most exciting event was triple coupon day at Stop & Shop. I had been to the city twice in my sheltered little life, once to pick up Dad's great-aunt on a train and once for a funeral.

North Prospect. Abbreviation = No. Prospect. More like NO Prospect. North Prospect, the land of the Whities. Just about everyone was either Catholic or Protestant and could trace their roots from somewhere in Europe. If you knew a Jew or an adopted Korean you were lucky. About the only chance you had for variety was which country your grandparents were from. People just rattled off fractions. I'm 1/2 Italian, 1/4 Irish, 1/8 German, 1/8 not sure. The only time you'd ever see enough Latino or black kids to count on two hands was when our basketball team played another school from the city.

Aunt Lydia and Aunt Nell were such fakes. Just like everyone else their age, they loved that this was Whitetown. They'd say things like of course I'm not racist, the KKK is just *awful*, because they knew that was what you were supposed to say in polite company. But then they'd drive their little minivans down their all-white streets and park in their safe little homogenized world. There was a grand total of one black family in our entire neighborhood, and they moved in a few houses down from us about five years ago.

At least that old lady I tried to sell Girl Scout cookies to wasn't a fake—there was no question where she stood on the issue. It was pretty pathetic how I'd only been a Girl Scout for one measly year. But frankly that was long enough considering we never got to do anything exciting like go camping or whittle with a real knife like the Boy Scouts did. It was completely sexist and unfair. No doubt Mr. Dobson would approve. He was probably a den master or ringleader or whatever you called them. Our Girl Scout activities consisted of making Christmas ornaments out of seashells and plaster of Paris or eating the Rice Krispy treats that someone's Mom had made. And our meetings were after school in the cafeteria, so the students who rode the late bus could gawk at you in your embarrassing uniform. I had been going door-to-door on the street behind my house, trying to sell some overpriced cookies so we could make five cents on the dollar. When that old lady in the yellow house came to the door, she stood there staring at me. You're the Sampson girl, aren't you? Yes. Didn't a black family move into the old Consiglio house down the street from you? When she said the word black, she leaned in toward me and whispered it, like she was revealing some huge secret that all zero people on the dead-end street were trying to hear. Even at ten years old, I knew what sort of lady I was dealing with. She couldn't hide the disgust on her face. But I didn't know what to say other than yes. She didn't buy any cookies, and I didn't have a snappy comeback. Failure on my part times two.

It just didn't make sense to have a town where everyone was the same, in my opinion. All from Europe, all white. Of course everyone claimed that suburbs like this evolved in the name of safety. And obviously I wouldn't want to live somewhere where I'd have to dodge stray gunfire, but it just made things so dull and unrealistic. America was supposed to be the great melting pot, but somebody forgot to throw anything into the North Prospect pot except for a few sorry potatoes.

Five

September

The Sampsons had termites.

Fitting, really. And I might have found it funny that the one Biblical plague Dad hadn't accounted for was upon us if we hadn't been forced to leave our house—or more specifically if I hadn't been forced to leave my room. My sanctuary. Our resident entomologist discovered them.

"I found a bug," Ben announced at dinner one night.

He pointed to the kitchen windowsill, but no one paid much attention to this until fidgety Ryan got bored with dinner and went over to investigate.

"Hey, he's not kidding. Check this out, they're dead ants," Ryan said. Ben joined him at the window.

"Fascinating," I said.

"Come finish your dinner, please," Dad said.

"They've got wings," Ryan said.

Dad sprang up as if he had just sat down on something very sharp.

"Look," Ryan said.

"Oh good God," Dad said.

"What is it?" Mom said.

I finally got up and joined in the fun. Two dead insects lay in the corner of the windowsill next to a small pile of sawdust, their thin wings stretched out behind their dark bodies.

"They're just some flying ants," Ryan said.

"They aren't flying ants. They're termites," Dad said.

"Termites!" Ben said.

"Oh boy," I said.

"Termites? We have termites? Cool," Ryan said.

"What are we going to do?" Mom said.

"Don't worry, it'll be fine. I'll go to Home Depot tomorrow and talk to someone. I'm sure I can just get some pesticide," Dad said.

"Oh, maybe they'll have to put one of those big circus tents over our house like they do on TV," Ryan said.

I held back what I was thinking: it would have been apropos for this circus of a family.

Dad did go to Home Depot the next day with the intention of getting a do-it-yourself solution, and he returned home with a business card from Old Salem Exterminators. No doubt he had run into some male employee his age and had immediately become submissive. I was surprised he hadn't walked out with some gardening supplies and a new drill to boot.

Of course as soon as he came home he started spewing all these facts to justify giving in to the professional (read: expensive) option. The concrete in the foundation will crack over time, and that creates openings for them to crawl through. Termites don't need much. They can squeeze through a crack one-fiftieth of an inch wide. Do-it-yourself will just be too difficult. You have to rent expensive equipment. It doesn't just take an hour, it takes a few days to do it properly. Old Salem Exterminators will give us a fair price, not like those commercial ones. It's family-owned.

I think the only person who needed convincing was Dad himself, and I don't know if he succeeded.

The day we had to vacate our house, Ryan, Ben, and I we were all stalling, perhaps thinking if we wasted enough time we would somehow be granted permission to stay behind with the bugs and the fumes. Ben especially did not want to leave. Anthony, our exterminator, had become Ben's new best friend. If that guy got down on his hands and knees to look at something, Ben would too. Anthony was basically a superhero come to life for Ben. He killed scores of bugs all at once, forget about one at a time, and managed to get paid for it. (Although Ben never did kill any of the bugs he found, so you had to wonder if he was bothered at all by the termite slaughter.) And you could be sure Anthony was going to miss Ben, too. It was probably the first time in Anthony's life that anyone showed any interest in what he was doing, since exterminator was right up there with accountant on the excitement meter.

It really was sweet to see Ben so captivated by someone. I went outside to watch him for a bit instead of packing my bag.

Anthony was kneeling on the ground and Ben was standing behind him holding a black tool shaped like a "T." Ben was being very quiet and attentive, which was unlike him. You wouldn't exactly classify him as the studious kind, and yet he might as well be holding a pen and notebook as he observed Anthony. In fact, he hadn't made any of his noises around him.

I walked up to Ben. "Having fun?"

"I think he is. I've got myself a great helper here," Anthony said.

"We saw the termites," Ben said.

"We sure did. You have quite an infestation," Anthony said. "Ben, hand me that auger, please."

Ben came forward and solemnly gave the tool to Anthony.

"So what you are doing?" I said.

"I'm creating an insecticide barrier around your house as a repellant. And I'll be injecting some termiticide into the soil, and drilling some holes in the foundation and injecting some there as well."

Ben seemed enthralled. I raised my eyebrows and nodded at him as if to say, pretty impressive, isn't it?

"And you'll have this nice protective barrier when they're all done. It'll protect your house for at least seven years, probably more."

"Sounds good to me," I said. I would be long gone by then.

After dinner we packed up all the perishables as Dad called them (the cans in the pantry would be safe—they could survive all of the Biblical plagues!) and dragged ourselves to Aunt Lydia's. Nobody else could accommodate our bloated family, and of course a pricey hotel room was out of the question, so we had to go to the one place that would take us in. No room at the inn, so we were stuck in the stable. I did feel for poor Ben as he waved goodbye to his superhero. But of course he got right into the car without complaint.

Going to Aunt Lydia's was yet another activity I had no interest in doing and had no control over. They were coming at me from all angles—our trip to Disney was fast approaching and I still hadn't figured a way out of it. Getting my car and my license had been anticlimactic, to say the least. Even though I had been a model student in my driver's ed class and had passed the written and driving tests with flying colors, it didn't matter to them. I don't know what made me think they would change their behavior. Dad wouldn't let me drive anywhere except around the block. What a shift it would be when I finally just drove off one warm August morning to my new life. If that meant I couldn't drive to the mall now, I would just have to accept it as a tradeoff. Passive resistance, take thirty-seven.

The next day after school, Ryan and I were sitting in front of Aunt Lydia's TV. I was doing homework and Ryan was supposedly doing homework, but he was paying more attention to the TV. I prided myself on being able to concentrate while surrounded by commotion. That was one skill I could attribute to growing up as a Sampson.

Ben and Mom came into the room, and Ben sat down directly in front of the TV and starting playing with his He-Man. It was funny, Ben was very particular about his figures. He only played with He-Man and none of the others they'd bought for him. He even snubbed He-Man's friends. He only liked the protagonist.

"Did you do your homework already?" Mom said to Ryan.

"Yes."

"I really don't want Ben watching all that television," Mom said.

"OK," I said.

"You did all of it?" Mom said.

"Yes. I only had English. I did math in study hall," Ryan said.

"Let me see it."

Ryan took his essay off the coffee table and handed it to her. I had to admit I was now slightly interested in this, so I watched her eyes. They started out at a normal reading pace, but then they began to move faster and faster until they seemed to travel in a straight line to the bottom of the page. She read the second page in about three seconds.

"You didn't even read this book," she said.

"So? You never read it either. Who wants to read about boring mockingbirds?" Ryan said.

"'It is very obvious that Scout changes in many ways during the course of the novel.'"

"It is."

"'Big changes, smaller changes, a myriad of changes that come together to prove her fate in the end. It is also clear that the other minor characters, such as Jem and Boo Radley, change as well, although not as drastically as Scout. Her changes are the most important and obvious, essential in fact, and it is clear by the end of the novel that she is a new person in many fascinating ways.'"

"That's all true."

She gave Ryan an exasperated look and then flipped to the next page. "'Consequently, the author, Mrs. Harper Lee, creates a newly imagined Scout who captures our attention, and I defend Mrs. Lee's choices in this novel, *To Kill a Mockingbird*.'"

Then she just looked at him.

"So? That's not all of it. There's more that you didn't read. And Ms. Vogel only gave us like three weeks to finish the whole book. That's crazy. You can't expect someone to have two months off from school and then suddenly read an entire book in three weeks," Ryan said. "Look Mom, I spelled everything right and I used grammatically correct sentences. It's enough to pass."

She just kept staring at him, but I knew that he was speaking the truth. He had devised his own way to play the game—if nothing else at least he understood that the game existed. No doubt that was how he had managed to avoid reading any books and still earn C's. This was probably his boilerplate essay that could be used for any novel. Just plug in the names. But Ryan could obviously write, so his teachers couldn't fail him. It was easy to simply pass. You just had to sprinkle some myriads and consequentlys into the essay and presto, a C.

And of course English classes were ridiculous—see my erroneous B as proof positive. You started off reading some invented story, and then you had to conjure up some arbitrary thesis for your essay, which you then had to fill with whatever outlandish gobbledygook you thought the teacher would like. Some teachers loved symbolism, others misogyny or Christ figures. It was preposterous, some of my former essays that were returned with big fat A's. These characters symbolized Adam and Eve, this other one was the evil snake, here was the Garden of Eden, and don't forget the tempting apple. Instant A.

Just then I happened to look over at Ben. He had stopped playing with his He-Man figure and was now digging his finger into the carpet. He kept scratching at whatever he saw there, his fuzzball gently shaking back and forth.

"What, Mom?" Ryan said.

She really could stare at a person forever without talking.

"You're starting off tenth grade with a terrible attitude. What about that D?"

"I got a C+ in English last year."

"And Mrs. Harper Lee? Shouldn't it be Mr.?"

I burst out laughing. Actually I think the only word that could properly describe the noise I made was a guffaw. They both looked over at me.

"Sorry, nothing," I said.

Cultural illiteracy abounds.

"No, that's right," Ryan said, unconvinced.

"Where's that book? I want you to read it." She was speaking quietly. She probably thought Aunt Lydia was listening.

"Fine."

"Don't you see how hard your sister works?"

"Don't bring me into this," I said.

"I want you to turn off this TV and go get that book now," Mom said.

"Why don't we first take Ben outside so we can all look for rocks to show Dad. We've never looked in this yard before. Want to go, Ben?" I said.

"Yeah." He took his hand out of the carpet and stood up.

Ryan didn't thank me for intervening when we got outside, but I didn't care since I hadn't done it for him anyway. Ben understood more than people realized, and rooting around in a carpet didn't seem like your ideal reaction.

I found a few rocks and then went over to see what Ben was up to. He had collected about ten, but half of them looked like chunks of concrete. I leaned in for a closer look and then put my hand on his shoulder, but he darted away from me like a little silver fish.

No affection, just like the rest of us. As if he were allergic to it. It was a Sampson trait. That was fine with me, though. Shelly's Mom was always telling her that she loved her, and Shelly said it every time they talked on the phone. Can I have Hannah over for dinner? OK I love you. Come pick me up, love you.

Our parents signed our birthday cards with love, but that was about it. But so what? Nobody wanted to see public displays of affection—it made everyone uncomfortable. Sometimes you'd even see older kids holding their parent's hand in public. So embarrassing. At least I didn't have to deal with that.

"Which rock is your favorite?" I said.

He came over and pointed to the largest rock.

Then he suddenly started to do his dog. He squatted down and hopped toward me, which made him look more like a kangaroo than a dog. Every time he hopped, he did a really great impression of a dog barking, and after a few seconds I started laughing. I couldn't help it. His imitation was so good you would swear he was hiding an actual dog somewhere nearby.

"Hey Rover."

He growled at me.

"You ready to go inside?"

"Yeah." He stood back up.

Ryan was clearly still smarting over his Mr. Harper Lee incident and had been more focused on kicking rocks than collecting any. Ben and I wiped most of the dirt off the rocks we had collected and brought them into the kitchen. Ryan eventually trudged along behind us. Dad and Aunt Lydia were in there, and they looked startled when we came into the room, as if they had forgotten they had invited the children here as well.

"Do we need to put these dirty stones on the kitchen table?" Aunt Lydia said.

"They're for Dad to look at," I said.

"Here, let's take them outside," Dad said.

Aunt Lydia glared at the rocks and then puckered up her mouth the way people do right before they're going to vomit. Which made sense, since I had put a pile of dead slugs on the table. Oh wait, it was just some rocks.

Dad wet a paper towel and wiped the table clear of all seven specks of dirt that were there.

"Let's see what you've found," Dad said when we got outside.

"Why does she hate us?" I said.

Dad kept looking down at the rocks. He was trying to brush the non-existent dirt off them.

"She doesn't hate you. Don't say that. Let's hose these off, we'll be able to see them better that way."

Dad turned on the hose, and I gave Ben the nozzle end. He pointed the stream of water at the rocks, moving it around in a slow circle to wet them all. He excelled at tasks like that. So serious.

"We didn't make a mess on the table. We cleaned them off before we brought them in. Why does she care?" I said.

Dad didn't say anything. I really don't know why I cared, either. But I did—or at least was slightly interested to know why someone would be this hostile toward me. It had to be more than her usual resentment of my boldness, for being an ungirl in her 1950's playbook.

"And you've been a rock collector for years. She has to be used to them by now," I said.

"Don't worry about her. She's not mad, that's just her way," Dad said. "Well, I think you found some sandstone here. This is granite, which is formed when molten lava, called magma, slowly cools under the earth's crust."

Ben kept the water there, even though Dad was touching the rocks.

"What's this big flat one?" I said.

"That's actually marble, the same kind you might find in statues or on smooth floors. It's formed when limestone is under a lot of pressure and high temperatures. You get a much harder and smoother rock, which is why it's so valuable," Dad said.

"That's Ben's favorite one," I said.

"Yeah, my favorite," Ben said.

"Let's leave them here and go back inside for dinner. Hannah, shut the water off, please," Dad said.

"You don't want to keep any of them?" I said. When I was younger, he would always select at least one rock to keep. I guess I just wanted him to humor me for old time's sake. Or maybe I wanted a bit of sweetness to offset Aunt Lydia's bite.

Dad shook the water off the piece of marble and put it in his pocket. He really had to struggle to fit it in there.

"This is a good one for my collection," he said. "Let's go in for dinner."

Obviously Aunt Lydia did not have any of Ben's juice boxes or chicken nuggets—she probably didn't even have one measly frozen pizza in the whole house. But Dad must have either stopped at the store after work or packed them in with the seventeen thousand other food items we'd lugged over with us. The rest of us were stuck with a fabulous assortment of Mom's leftover meatloaf, a few stale potato chip crumbs, some Beanie Weanies (a name the Sampsons had coined for a can of baked beans with some cut-up hot dogs thrown in), half a pot of hard Rice-A-Roni, and some of Aunt Lydia's mashed potatoes. Even though I'd never admit it to her face, the woman could make a mean batch of potatoes. But how hard was it to make mashed potatoes? She probably just cheated and threw a whole stick of butter in there to make it look like she was some gourmet chef. What didn't taste good with butter?

Aunt Lydia looked over at Ben, and for a minute I thought she was going to repeat her melancholy staring again. I had seen her do it a second time at Nonnie's birthday picnic last month. But she stopped looking at him after a few moments and turned to Dad.

"Does he want any of these potatoes? Or the meatloaf?" Aunt Lydia said.

"Sorry Lydia. But this is all he'll eat," Dad said. He was heating up the chicken nuggets in the microwave.

"Maybe he should try something new. It isn't right to have a diet with no variety," Aunt Lydia said.

"He won't eat it," I said.

"Well, maybe he should try," Aunt Lydia said.

"He won't eat it. He won't throw a fit or anything, he just won't eat it," I said. What was she, deaf?

She turned to Dad. "Sit down. I'll heat them up."

Then we all just sat there and ate our food in uncomfortable silence. The only thing missing was Uncle Reginald's exciting company. He was out driving his big bad truck. Although no one, his wife included, would have even noticed if he were here. At least when Mom and Dad walked past each other, one of them would move to the side to make room, maybe put a hand on the other's shoulder. After you, Sue. Or Dad would notice if Mom's cup was low on coffee and fill it up for her. But Uncle Reginald and Aunt Lydia just kind of glided past each other, without so much as brushing up against the other's sleeve. It was as if someone had choreographed the whole sequence for them.

I looked around the room to see if anything had been added since I was last here. This house was just as extreme as ours, but the polar opposite. The whole place was essentially bare—our basement put it to shame. It was as if Aunt Lydia had gone around and collected all the typical items that people needed to furnish a house and hid them in a big box, and then randomly selected a few to put out on display. One dishrag on the counter. One nondescript magnet on the refrigerator. Finding a trash can was like a scavenger hunt. She had to be hiding that darn box somewhere.

But no alcohol. That was the one thing I knew she wasn't hiding. The Sampsons were totally dry across the board, with one glaring exception. There wasn't even a sad little bottle of wine from somebody's wedding in our entire house. I could understand why they didn't have any here, with Cousin Eddie and all, but why not us? I'd love to see Dad get drunk just once, to lose control or if nothing else at least get a little silly. You could tell he had it in him, somewhere.

"Have you checked your smoke detectors lately? You should change the batteries during daylight savings time. That's coming up soon," Dad said.

"I think Reg changes them," Aunt Lydia said.

"You're going to read that book after dinner," Mom said quietly.

"Fine," Ryan said.

"What book?" Dad said.

"*To Bore a Mockingbird*," Ryan said.

"Can I go upstairs and do my homework?" I said.

"No, eat your dinner," Dad said.

"I'm finished," Ryan said. He had barely touched anything on his plate. His glob of Beanie Weanies had begun to form a suspicious layer of oily film.

"Everyone is staying here," Dad said.

Frankly I started to get pretty annoyed at this point. I was being held captive by these people, and for what? I had to trade bettering my mind with books for listening to them drone on about smoke detectors, which only stoked my feelings of powerlessness.

"So can we go to Boston this spring?" I said.

"What for?" Dad said.

"To visit colleges. Most people wait until the summer, but I'd like to get a head start and see the school when the students are actually around. I need to go to Washington D.C., too."

"I'm not sure. We'll have to talk about it," Dad said. He flashed me a look of impatience.

"Boston is a lot closer than Orlando," I said.

"We'll try, Hannah," Mom said.

"I'll just go by myself then. That's fine with me," I said.

"No, you won't be doing that," Dad said.

"You can't just peruse a pamphlet and then apply. I have to visit these schools. No, I'm going to visit these schools," I said.

Dad and Mom looked at me not with anger but rather pleading misery. And so I stopped. Of course I knew what I was doing—I was punishing them for making me stay at the table, publically airing our family's private conversations which I knew would make them squirm. But I was a wimp. I couldn't punish them that severely.

Aunt Lydia had decided to join the glare-at-Hannah game as well. But after the phantom dirt on the table incident, I had to wonder if I was really the source of her anger. Maybe what she wanted more than anything was for someone to finally ask about him. Maybe she just wanted to talk about her lost son. And she was angry that no one had the guts to do it, especially someone like me who could be assertive at times. What would happen if I just came out and said, so what's the latest on Eddie? Or did she never want to hear his name again?

Had he made her fundamentally miserable?

Dad let us all escape to the living room after a couple more minutes of strained silence broken up by a few mindless comments. Ben sat down on the floor and almost immediately began digging his finger into the carpet again, but this time he began to make these little noises, like he was trying to clear his throat in a high-pitched voice. He kept scratching at whatever he saw in the carpet and making those noises, and I kept thinking that I should probably be a little worried about him. Sure, all kids behaved strangely at times, but Ben was eight, not four. And he'd done his dog today. Of course, the normal way to find out if he was OK would be to just ask someone, but normal never seemed to show up to the party in my family, although denial was certainly in attendance. And Ryan couldn't focus on anything for more than ten seconds. Although I could at least see why a teenage boy wouldn't notice or care. But his own parents? When that school worker tried to have Ben tested for a learning disability, Mom just about flipped. And Dad let Mom call all the shots with Ben. I was pretty sure that was why she had taken a job at Ben's school. She was probably always on the lookout and ready to run interference if the teachers tried any funny stuff with him. She wouldn't even notice if they put me in an insane asylum. Or else she'd just take some pictures for the Hannah in the Loony Bin scrapbook page. Here's Hannah in her straightjacket. Oh, how darling.

I put down my book. "Hey Ben, let's go look where those old games are. We can find something to play."

He took his hand out of the carpet. "Yeah."

We knelt down in front of the cabinet, where there were all the usual suspects—Monopoly, Clue, Risk, Scrabble—in battered boxes. Dad had been kind enough to show them to us once when we were bored out of our minds. It did feel strange looking at these worn games that were once played by a relative I'd never met and knew so little about. It was almost scandalous, touching a drug addict's childhood things.

I suddenly wanted to play Monopoly. Or more precisely, I wanted to beat Dad at Monopoly. I deserved a stunning, public victory after being forced to sit through that dinner. I envisioned this cutthroat match, with everyone staring at the dice in anticipation to see if Hannah or Dad was going to take Boardwalk. Plus, Dad would obviously be the bank, and I hated being the bank. You couldn't pay attention to the game because every ten seconds someone was pestering you for their two hundred dollars for passing Go. Dad would always grow so serious when he was the bank. When he gave you your change from a transaction, he would count it back to you like a darn grocery store clerk. OK, Marvin Gardens, that's two sixty. Out of five? Here's forty which makes three, four, and five makes five hundred. I was surprised he didn't wear his monocle when he was the bank. I couldn't remember the last time we had all played Monopoly together. Then again, it was somewhat of a challenge when your set was missing all of the fifties and about half of the little green houses.

"Want to see if we can get Ryan and Dad to play this?" I said, pointing to Monopoly.

"Too hard."

"You can be on my team, OK? We'll beat everyone."

"Yeah."

We went in the kitchen, but Mom was the only one in there. She was sitting at the table enlightening herself with the *Gazette*.

"Mom, do you want to play Monopoly with us?" I said, knowing full well she wouldn't.

"I'm going to bed soon, my head is bothering me. Ask your father."

"Where is he?"

"I don't know."

I turned around.

"Dad," I said.

"Hannah, please. My head."

"I wasn't loud." I wasn't, either. I was quiet on purpose—I wasn't insensitive or cruel. Sometimes it seemed that her default position with me was pure defense.

Ben and I went back into the living room and then partway up the stairs.

"Dad," I said.

"Not up here," Ryan said.

"Let's go see if he'll play," I said.

"Ryan!" Ben said. He ran in front of me. "Ryan!"

He was sitting on the bed with *To Kill a Mockingbird* face down on the covers, unread. Instead he was playing a handheld video game. On the silent setting, of course.

"Ryan," Ben said, pointing to Monopoly. "Come play."

"I'm busy." He didn't take his eyes off the screen.

"Right, we can see that. Sorry to interrupt," I said.

He finally looked up. "Ben can't play that."

"He's on my team. Dad even said he'd play," I said.

"If Dad's playing then you already have enough players. And Monopoly's so boring anyway. The whole game's decided right away by whatever you roll the first time around the board."

He was right. By the first go-around you basically knew who would win, and there were times when I'd gotten the dregs of the real estate market and wanted to quit at that point. So I wasn't going to push it with Ryan. Frankly, I was already starting to lose interest, but I still would have liked to beat Dad. And it would give Ben something to do.

"Fine, who needs you. Let's go get Dad, Ben," I said.

We went back into the kitchen, and Mom told us to try the basement. We found him down there with Aunt Lydia looking at a water stain on the ceiling that was shaped like a mangled octopus.

"Dad," I said.

He held up his hand, so we just stood there and waited for Aunt Lydia to stop taking advantage of him. He was always stuck doing her crap because Uncle Reginald was so incompetent. Well, I suppose the man was a decent driver, or else we would've found out by now. But if it wasn't for Dad, this house would have fallen down already. Not like my father was Bob Vila or anything. Even though he attempted to fix everything, Dad had never properly fixed a single thing. It was at the point now where I wouldn't even tell him if something was broken. This doorknob? Loose? No, it's fine. Couldn't be better. I'd rather deal with it broken than with one of Dad's "solutions." He couldn't even fix that handle on the inside of Mom's car that kept pulling away from the door whenever you tried to close it. He ended up jury-rigging it with copious amounts of duct tape, and now whenever I closed the door, it felt like I was clutching a wad of already chewed gum. I could only imagine the disaster of a house we'd be left with if we hadn't hired Anthony. But whatever solution Dad came up with, you could count on one thing: it would somehow involve duct tape. He was obsessed with the stuff, used it for everything. Duct tape on the pool deck chair, clutching its broken arm a little too tightly. On Dad's loose rearview mirror where it connected to the windshield. And who could forget the time he tried to duct tape the side of his eyeglasses? Luckily Ryan and I caught him in the act and convinced him to stop. We told him we would never be seen in public with him again.

But Aunt Lydia had no choice, and neither did Dad. He had to be her handyman. Dad was like me but opposite: the only boy, surrounded by sisters on all sides. Either way you were a little screwed.

I nudged Ben, since we had waited patiently long enough. They had probably forgotten we were even standing there.

"Come play," Ben said.

Dad was still looking at the blotchy octopus and muttering a few things to Aunt Lydia.

"Dad," I said.

They both looked as us.

"Hmm?" Dad said.

Ben flung his hand out and hit the Monopoly box while saying the letter "z" quickly.

"I'm sorry kids, I've got to look at this. You two play."

But now I had a bigger problem than Dad not wanting to play. Aunt Lydia was staring at the Monopoly box. Then she looked up at me, and her eyes asked how I dare even think about touching her son's game. Any sympathy I might have had for her vanished when I saw the disdain there. I clutched Monopoly to my stomach and stared back at her.

"Why can't Uncle Reginald fix that? You come play with us."

My little barb was pointless. She said nothing in response and Dad was clearly warning me with his body language, so we gave up the whole idea of playing a game and just returned to the living room. It was pretty sad, if you asked me. Here we were, about to go to the Happiest Place on Earth, and we couldn't even manage to play one measly game of Monopoly together.

Oh well, Ben, I wanted to say. I tried but you're back on your own. Enjoy digging in the carpet.

Finally I decided to just go to bed early and end this exciting day. Ryan had claimed the bed while I was trying to help our younger brother, so I was relegated to the floor. My luxurious accommodations were a paper-thin pillow and a scratchy sleeping bag, circa 1932. It had a picture of Crayola Crayons on it, for God's sake.

But I couldn't fall asleep. First of all, it was approximately one hundred degrees in there, and my ideal sleeping conditions were a nice cool room with lots of covers to snuggle under. And I wasn't about to lie on top of the sleeping bag, because it was made out of sandpaper. The other problem was that Ryan was breathing loudly. I also needed total quiet to fall asleep.

I kept switching positions, going from my left side to my back and then to my right side, but I still couldn't sleep. So instead I started thinking about how this could have been his room. He could have done his homework or gotten ready for school right here. I couldn't get a clear picture of him in my head, because I had only seen a handful of photos of him in my old scrapbooks. I certainly wouldn't find any pictures lying around this shell of a house. I wondered if they would rather have him dead than the uncertainty of wondering if he was out there somewhere, stealing and dirty and homeless. What would I want? If he was alive, then there was always that little bit of hope that one day he could just come walking back through the door, wearing a clean suit and announcing: Hi everyone, I'm home. The prodigal son, who got a juicy goat slaughtered for him when he came back home after blowing all of his inheritance on blackjack. (Frankly that story had always annoyed me, since I was clearly the good son toiling away in the fields.

No sumptuous goat feast for me.) But the odds on that were about a million to one. The hope was probably worse than just knowing he never could return. That hope would hurt more than relieve, it would always be there like a foreign object in your eye that you couldn't see but could feel scratching away at it, day after day. I was never having kids. Once they were out there, you had to spend your whole life worrying about them. You became vulnerable the second they were born. It wasn't worth it.

The alarm finally went off. I had only been watching it for the past hour.

"Thanks a lot for yelling last night," I said.

"What are you talking about?" Ryan said.

"You yelled something in your sleep. You must've been having a nightmare."

"I did not."

"Yes you did. It was like, 'just stop it' or 'you have to stop it.' And right when I was about to fall asleep in this boiler room. I think I slept for a total of thirty minutes. What were you dreaming about?"

"I don't know. I never remember any of my dreams."

"Hey, maybe this room is haunted," I said.

"It is kind of spooky, isn't it?"

"It is strange to think that one of our relatives is out there on the streets eating out of a dumpster or in a mental institution."

"We should sneak him into our basement. All he'd need is your sleeping bag and a can opener."

I laughed. "He could do us a favor and eat all the unlabeled ones."

"Dad would go, 'Now, I just know we had more than these. Where are my twenty-nine-cent unlabeleds? There was quite a number of them here the other day.'"

I laughed again.

"How long do you think somebody could live down there on those cans?" Ryan said.

"I'd guess twenty years. But they'd probably die from high

blood pressure first."

"Why?"

"Those cans are full of salt. Salt is a preservative."

"Oh."

For some reason, I felt like asking him about Ben. Maybe it was my lack of sleep or his morning grogginess, which gave him an unusual air of seriousness, that made me think there was any point in bringing it up.

"Do you ever worry about Ben?"

Ryan shrugged. "He'll be fine."

"Probably. But what if he's not?"

"He'll grow out of it. He's a kid. They're all crazy."

"Yeah, what could we do about it, anyway? We aren't child psychiatrists."

"Exactly. I'm getting up now. This room smells like mothballs."

Six

October

Asylum (n) sanctuary, shelter; place of refuge

Disney World is an asylum.

Punctual (adj) arriving or taking place exactly at the arranged time; prompt

Their ridiculously early flight did not prevent the ever-punctual Sampsons from making it to the airport with time to spare. We had then been able to spend the rest of the day spinning on human-sized teacups and crawling down pseudo rivers on uncomfortable boats. Only my family would find a way to dive right into the parks and successfully rush our way through Day One. It was easy if you woke up at 4:00 a.m. Punctual.

Allay (v) to calm or reduce the intensity of; relieve

The airline chose to show some God-awful Disney movie to allay our boredom during the flight. The perfect segue into the Land of Never-Never. Although I had been sure it wouldn't matter to the Sampsons. There were only two possibilities as to why Dad had willingly forked over five dollars apiece for the headsets. One: He had put on his we're-on-vacation-let's-throw-caution-to-the-wind hat, where he would suddenly become a spendthrift (another good SAT word, with the appearance of thrift throwing many an unprepared test-taker off track). He would wear the hat for only a couple of minutes at a time, so you really had to ply him with requests before the window slammed shut. Or two: He had done a quick cost-benefit analysis and realized it was worth the fifteen bucks to sedate us—or allay our boredom—for most of the trip by having us watch a movie. But it had helped the time go by. Between the cokes, the peanuts, and the mindless crap on the grainy screen, we were there in no time. It was quite prosaic ((adj) boring, dull; lacking imagination) that the only flight path I'd ever followed was the one from Hartford to Orlando.

Ubiquitous (adj) being or seeming to be present everywhere

As we were awaiting the arrival of our luggage, I had to take issue with the sign attached to the ubiquitous black suitcase in the middle of the conveyor belt that said: Please check your tags, as many bags look alike. Au contraire. Our luggage was held together by reams of duct tape, as if it were trying to dupe the twenty-year-old suitcases into believing they were actually energetic five-year-olds who could easily do another trip. Here's to duct tape, that magical youth elixir. Needless to say, we had no trouble spotting our luggage. Not *all* bags look alike.

I had another one: Classy (adj) opposite of this hotel. Because our morally upright father refused to lie about the number of people staying in our room, our hotel choices were quite limited, since reserving two rooms would have been too expensive. So we ended up with a real gem. Or should I say scam. It was no more than a room for four with a cot thrown in.

"Hannah, turn the stupid light off. I want to go to sleep," Ryan whispered.

"I'm studying."

"If I have to take the cot, then I should get to decide when to turn off the lights. I'm tired."

"Just close your eyes. Everyone else fell asleep with no problem."

"I'm getting up and turning it off."

"Fine."

I switched off the lamp.

When I woke up, Ryan and Ben were still asleep. I walked

toward the kitchen, but stopped suddenly in the doorway.

They were already starting with their frugal games. And at seven in the morning to boot. One of them must have gone out at the crack of dawn to buy the ingredients. Although this way was probably the least painful, seeing that every time we tried to do something as simple as feeding ourselves, it inevitably turned into a typical Sampson disaster.

They had created their two-person assembly line with Dad at the helm. He was silently laying slices of bread onto the paper-towel-covered counter, dealing them out like a deck of cards. Then Mom began to spread a layer of peanut butter onto the first slice. Probably not the best choice for the job—she always handled the knife too roughly, so without fail the Wonder bread, which was about as sturdy as a fluffy white cloud, would tear and clot as the peanut butter passed over it. As soon as she finished with the first piece, Dad started on its pair. He had two jars uncapped and waiting, and he took turns dipping his knife into the grape and strawberry jellies and smearing them onto the bread, being careful to always stay one slice behind his wife. Once she had reached the end of the line, Mom moved behind Dad and started to close up the sandwiches. Dad finished with the jelly application and then went to get the box of plastic bags. Not the zip lock kind of course, because those cost three times as much, but the ones with the fold-over flap. He bagged the sandwiches, and then they both stacked them into the infamous diaper bag.

No matter how many times I'd seen it, I couldn't help but be slightly mesmerized by the whole process. It was so well orchestrated, such a strange ritual. Like something you might see on an Animal Kingdom documentary. I almost felt guilty for witnessing it.

I cleared my throat loudly, in case they hadn't realized I was standing there.

"Do we have any orange juice?" I said.

"Yes. But first go wake up your brothers for me, please," Mom said.

After breakfast, it took us a good forty-five minutes and two false starts—one because Mom noticed that Ben didn't have his hat (that Florida sun is harsh) and the other because Ryan realized he'd sat on a chocolate donut at some point this morning—before we were able to leave our hotel room. We were walking through the lobby when a man dressed like a destitute newspaper reporter from the 1920's approached Dad.

"Excuse me, sir. Would you like two free passes to Typhoon Lagoon?" the reporter said.

"Yes," Ryan said.

"Shh. What's the catch?" Dad said.

"There's no catch. All you and your family have to do is take a tour of our timeshare and attend a two-hour presentation, and they're yours. There's no obligation to buy whatsoever."

You could just see the gears turning in his accountant head as he weighed (c) cost of wasted time/money against (v) value of tickets. We'd lose about a half a day, so he should include the car and hotel in his estimate, if he was smart, plus the lost time at the parks.

"Thank you, but we'll pass," Dad said.

Well done, oh sagacious one.

Everyone piled into the rental car. Theme park of the day: EPCOT. We had patronized the Magic Kingdom yesterday. Or more accurately it had patronized us. With infantile rides like Snow White's Scary Adventures. But EPCOT I could tolerate. I could endure. Abide. Whoever designed EPCOT at least took a stab at science and put some watered-down facts in there. Somewhere. It was like one of those Waldo books: *Find Science Now*. The end product was a theme park best suited for older children and possibly illiterate adults.

It was barely acceptable to come to Disney World even once. Therefore, visit number two for me could be classified as . . .truly inane. Good SAT word. If the Magic Kingdom was any indication, nothing much had changed since the last time we were here. Sure they had added a few rides, but they never seemed to update any of the others. So why did people keep coming back again and again? Did they forget what it was like the first time?

As soon as we walked through the front gates, Ben started pointing at the big golf ball, as Ryan called it. He wasn't the only one who wanted to ride it—at least half of the kids around us were trying to drag their parents toward it. But it wasn't their fault. That golf ball was clearly propaganda. Disney put a gargantuan sphere right at the entrance so we would all be forced to drool over it the moment we entered the park. And everywhere you turned they were selling T-shirts, postcards, beach towels, and mugs with that golf ball plastered all over them so that people would take them back to their hometowns where their neighbors would see the beach towel hanging on the clothesline and experience such golf ball envy that they'd feel the need to come here and buy two towels and a mug to best their neighbor. Propaganda.

The line for the golf ball was already long, but we took our ten mandatory pictures in front of it and then joined the swarm anyway. Just like Pavlov's dogs.

I took my list of words out of my pocket.

Hackneyed (adj) clichéd, worn out by overuse

What hackneyed theatrics await me in this giant golf ball? Hackneyed. Clichéd. How could I remember it? Hack. I'd like to hack those clichés. No, that was stupid.

Another appropriate one:

Hedonist (n) one who pursues pleasure as a goal

Disney World is chock-full of hedonists willing to wait in long lines for just a few moments of entertainment. So what if there are wars, poverty, and diseases out there? There's still pleasure to be had here, regardless of what's going on in the real world. Hedonist. It was like the H's were just tailor-made for Disney World.

I had to remember that my verbal PSAT score was almost two hundred points below my goal. It didn't matter if studying these words was boring. No, if this was a mundane endeavor. I had to up my score.

"Why don't they give us a movie to watch or something? I'm already tired of waiting in lines, and it's only the second day," Ryan said.

I looked down at the list. "Are you saying that these lines

exasperate you? Or maybe you're so puerile you can't wait patiently like a big boy?"

He glanced over at the list. "And you are so superfluous."

"That's not even how you pronounce that word. Nice job." He said it like the super of a building.

"Like you're ever going to use any these words after the test."

I looked down. Better go back to the beginning.

Abate (v) to reduce in amount or intensity; lessen

Our patience is abating as this wait drags on. The termites have abated the mass of my house. Abate. Lessen.

Abet (v) to aid, encourage, or help

I wish my Civic were here to abet me in my escape.

"Give me that stupid list. I'll make you remember some of these," Ryan said.

I handed it to him.

"Sometime today," I said.

"OK. I have two." He brought his fist close to his mouth, as if speaking into a microphone. "It doesn't take a *clairvoyant* to know this ride is going to suck. Consequently, Dad can be quite *parsimonious* when it comes to canned goods."

I smiled. Sometimes Ryan and I really did think alike.

"Put that away," Mom said.

"I'm learning," Ryan said.

"Not bad. But I already knew those two," I said.

"Now you do one. Do one about Aunt Lydia."

"No, I need to look them over now."

"Come on, just do one."

I took the list from him.

"Aunt Lydia's condescending attitude toward the Samson children is perfidious seeing that she is Dad's sister."

"What's perfidious?"

"Treacherous, disloyal."

"Ooh, good one!"

"That's enough of that game," Dad said. But it really did seem like he was holding back a smile. You could see it in his eyes. If Mom hadn't been there, I really think he would have laughed. Heck, maybe he would've even chipped in with an Uncle Reginald example of his own.

I looked down at the list, but Ryan tapped my arm.

"Would you go to college here? This far away?"

I kept looking down. Circuitous. How did you pronounce—

"What, now that you can drive I'm not allowed to speak to you anymore?"

"It's too hot. Who wants to sweat half the year? Besides, there aren't any good colleges in Florida. The closest is probably Emory." I looked back down.

I still didn't know what my first choice was. Probably BC, but until I took the tours I wouldn't really know. And the financial aid packages could change everything—I didn't want to be in debt forever if I could avoid it. If I didn't get into BC, I'd settle for Tufts. Although I'd probably be better off doing a state school. Tufts costs twice as much but definitely wasn't twice as good. UVA was definitely on the list. Thomas Jefferson did a good job with that one.

We finally reached the boarding area, where we would get to play a round of How Many in Your Party. I was tempted to reply, you call this a party? The problem was we had five people in our so-called party. This would throw the ride operators for a loop. When you answered five, they would give you this disappointed look, as if to say oh, couldn't you make do with one less person? It would be so much easier for us. And then they'd finally accept it and say five? Well, you're going to have to do two and three then. Two and three. As if they were trying to break us neatly in half but couldn't even do that. You know they really wanted to say four and one. Maroon Dad in a car by himself. There was a grand total of two rides so far that let all of us sit together. Disney World wanted you to have the perfect little four-person family. Not us fives. We crashed the system.

Mom and Dad went first, but only after I convinced them to let us take Ben. Our car immediately started climbing a steep hill, and then

Walter Cronkite's voice began to emanate from somewhere behind my left ear, practically lulling me to sleep. We passed a reenactment of a Neanderthal painting animal figures on a cave wall, and Cronkite informed the dolts in the audience who couldn't figure it out for themselves that it represented the beginning of human history. I was amazed they weren't rioting in the streets over Disney's acceptance of Darwinism. We were in the South, after all.

Then we skipped ahead about fifty thousand years to an Egyptian Pharaoh reading a parchment. What I found most ironic about these rides was that Disney spent a ridiculous amount of money on its robots—excuse me, animatronics, since the term robot must have sounded too prosaic, boring, dull, like my flight path. How they spent all this money on these contraptions, making every attempt to give them a realistic look and human-like movements, only to have them creep back and forth, back and forth. It was idiotic. The Pharaoh started off by bringing his parchment in for a closer look, which made perfect sense. But then he returned it to the original spot and brought it back in toward himself all over again. Why would someone as intelligent as the Pharaoh do that? He wouldn't. He saw it just fine the first time. Disney needed to slow Pharaoh's hand down. I mean, you could turn around and watch him bring that parchment to his face and then reset twice more before your car moved on to the next exhibit. The timing was all off.

"Boring," Ryan said.

"Yeah, boring," Ben said.

"Ryan," Dad said from the car in front of us.

"What, you aren't enjoying learning about our history?" I said.

"If I don't listen in school, why would I listen on my vacation?"

He had a valid point.

I put my hand on my pocket. I considered trying to read my words, but it was too dark. There should be newspaper cars for the people who didn't want to watch the ride but were dragged along for various reasons. They'd be amply lit. Maybe even soundproof. They'd probably fill up faster than the regular cars.

89

All of a sudden I saw a projectile fly toward Michelangelo's head. It hit the side of the poor guy's neck while he was lying on his back trying to paint the Sistine Chapel.

"Was that you?" I said, leaning forward. I was sitting on the right side, farthest away from the robots, and Ben was in the middle.

He didn't answer me, and then a few minutes later I saw another one land near Gutenberg and his printing press. Whatever he was throwing looked to be about the size of a marble. But it was so dark in there except for the one dim light pointed at the robots forever moving their parchments to and fro that there was no way to tell what it was.

Ben laughed as another one missed a robot and landed on the floor with a metallic clink. I leaned forward again, and this time I caught him holding his hand sideways and flicking his wrist, as if he were skimming a flat stone across a lake.

"Ryan." I'd figured it out. Pennies.

"Stop being a baby. Or else go sit in Mom and Dad's car. Here Ben."

Ben took the coin out of Ryan's hand and immediately flung it at our parents' car, as if he'd been planning it all along. Ryan and I laughed.

"Nice, Ben. Real subtle," I said.

"These stupid lap bars make it hard to throw," Ryan said.

"Fine, give me one," I said.

I could tell he'd handed me a quarter, not a penny, without looking down at it. If Dad only knew that his children were literally throwing money away. I reached my hand back as far as I could and hurled the coin toward an overzealous newsboy. Even though Cronkite had begun lecturing again, I could hear a loud clang. Ryan and Ben started to laugh as soon as it landed.

Mom stretched her neck around the side of her car like a turtle coming out of its shell.

"What's going on over there?" she said.

They were still laughing.

"Ryan! Hannah!" Dad said. His voice seemed to fill the golf ball.

Mom pulled her neck back into its shell as our cars rounded a bend.

"Be quiet Dad! I'm trying to enjoy this ride," Ryan said. Ben was still laughing.

"Ryan," Mom said, slightly quieter than Dad's broadcast.

We could not possibly have been more embarrassing and blatant if we'd tried. These other people had paid some exorbitant amount of money so they could sit here quietly and watch their little show. My family, however, chose to launch pennies at Michelangelo's head and scream at each other between cars.

"Another," Ben said. He held out his hand.

"How about you quit while you're ahead," I said to Ryan. "If they stop the ride and we're stuck in this golf ball because of your little game, I'm going to throw those pennies at you."

"Here Ben, be sure to make a wish before you throw. Try and hit that radio," Ryan said.

I just shook my head. He must've had half the U.S. mint in his bag. But Ben did seem to be enjoying it, so how angry could I really get?

They proceeded to hit some of the most acclaimed inventors of the twentieth century on the head and chest. When our car rotated 180 degrees and began traveling backward, it only encouraged them even them more—they were now barely pausing between throws. We approached Neil Armstrong heroically working away on the space shuttle, and Ben took aim and hit him right on the butt. Even I had to laugh at that. The shot of the day, and it belonged to Ben.

As we crawled toward the exit, we watched Mom and Dad step out of their car. They turned around and stared at us.

"Hi," Ben said as we slowly passed them.

They were focusing on Ryan now. We exited our car.

"Ryan," Dad said.

He ignored them as he left, half-skipping down the ramp.

Which frankly did take some balls.

He stopped and leaned against the railing, and Ben went up to him and held out his hand as if he was begging. Which he was, really. Ryan slapped him five, trying to play it off. It was a decent try. But they weren't fooled that easily.

"What were you throwing?" Dad said.

"What?" Ryan said.

"Ben, what did you throw?" Dad said.

"Oh, that's so low—" Ryan said.

"Pennies," Ben said.

"Well Ryan, that's very mature. I didn't see any other fourteen-year-olds throwing loose change at the robots. Did you?" Dad said.

"I saw a sixteen-year-old," Ryan said, glancing at me.

"We take you here, to this nice place, and you can't even behave," Dad said.

"That ride was boring. I can't sit through these historical things," Ryan said.

"You're going to have to," Dad said.

"Why am I always doing things I don't want to do?" Ryan said.

"Can we get off this ramp so people can actually leave the ride?" I said. If I hadn't said anything, they would have just stayed there indefinitely. It was incredible how oblivious they could be to anyone but themselves sometimes.

We moved down to the bottom of the ramp.

"You're sitting on a bench while we go on the next ride as punishment," Dad said.

"Why am I always the one getting yelled at?"

"I wonder why. Actually, I think everyone in this family knows the answer to that question. Should we ask them just to be sure?" Dad said.

See, right there. That was his problem. He didn't know how to just end it. This would go on ad nauseam because neither he nor Ryan could drop anything. My parents' only weapon was words—they never hit or grabbed arms. Never. They would just lecture, scold, and yell, even though they had never won a single victory with those methods. Not that Ryan didn't usually deserve getting yelled at. But hadn't they learned by now that it didn't work with him? They occasionally took away a privilege, but that had no effect either. Maybe they should have spanked him. As a child, of course. It was too late now.

We did a few more rides, and then we went to the World Showcase, the section of EPCOT that consisted of pavilions "showcasing" various countries. In reality just a bunch of overpriced restaurants and gaudy gift shops "hawking" ethnic food and trinkets. Before we were allowed to eat lunch, we had to locate a restroom so we could rid our hands of the thousands of germs that only Dad had the ability to detect. Then we spread out across two benches in Italy right next to Alfredo's Restaurant, where people who actually purchased their food went to eat. It was a good thing we'd brought our own peanut butter and jelly sandwiches. That and chicken fingers would have probably been a hard ethnic cuisine to place. Maybe the Nutritionally Defunct Pavilion?

Mom began passing out the sandwiches. I felt as if I shouldn't eat mine, knowing the hard work that went into making it.

"This World Showcase is so boring," Ryan said.

"This World Showcase is so stereotyped," I said. "Who knew the only thing Italians do is listen to 'O Solo Mio' while they eat spaghetti and meatballs? And if you're German, you obviously dance the polka. Half of it isn't even true."

"Yeah, I didn't know that Mexicans just hit piñatas all day. And you can buy your own to whack for just 19.99," Ryan said.

"Hannah, stop questioning everything. Just try to enjoy it," Dad said.

Stop questioning everything. I think Dad was just quoting Socrates there. Didn't he say that? My fellow Greeks, stop questioning everything. Just enjoy. Enjoy EPCOT.

"OK, I won't point out that Africa, the second largest continent on the planet, isn't even represented here," I said.

"We've heard enough of your opinion on the matter. Can you please just let your younger brother enjoy this?" Dad said.

Sure. I could keep the truth to myself. Socrates and I were kindred spirits. Perhaps Dad had some hemlock for me to drink?

"Did you bring any canned peaches for dessert?" Ryan said.

I laughed.

"OK, very funny," Dad said.

"Seriously, I know Ben likes peanut butter and jelly, but can't he just have it himself? We could all have something else, like turkey and Swiss. Or egg salad. Mix it up a little," Ryan said.

"Everyone likes peanut butter and jelly," Mom said.

"I don't want peanut butter and jelly, I can have that any day. This is vacation. I'm going to find a hamburger," Ryan said.

"Sit down," Dad said.

"Why? I have my own money," Ryan said.

"No. Michelangelo has it all now," I said.

"Eat what we brought. A hamburger will cost ten times what this sandwich cost to make," Dad said.

"So? It's my money. I can spend it how I want," Ryan said.

"Should you give me money for rent then? Or for your plane ticket here?" Dad said.

"Just eat the stupid sandwich," I said.

But clearly that was too difficult for him to do. His take on my patented passive resistance: feeding his sandwich to the shrieking birds that were now flocking around us. Cacophony (n) a combination of harsh or discordant sounds. Dad was getting more and more angry, but at least by only offering PB&J to the wildlife instead of one of those pricey hamburgers, he was saving Dad's blood pressure a couple of points. Covert (adj) not in the open. Ryan was trying to be covert when throwing those pieces of bread. He was attempting to flick his hand as little as possible. However, his covert operation was rather overt, as those birds would come screaming at us with each dropped crumb.

"Ryan, stop wasting perfectly good food. There are a lot of children worse off than you in the world who would certainly like that sandwich," Dad said.

Like those children in Africa. But where were they . . . .

"I know that. Don't you think I know that?" Ryan said.

"Then stop throwing it," Dad said.

"All right, I won't do it anymore."

But then those birds would give him away.

I could understand why he did it. There was something fascinating about seeing a flock of birds fly in unison toward a piece of bread. You controlled their movements. You got to be God for a moment. And if you were really good at it, like Ryan was, you could make it so they caught the food directly in their mouths. Awesome powers.

By the end of the day, Dad finally broke down and bought us all an ice cream from the carts. You could see the obvious pain on his face when he had to shell out twenty bucks and barely receive any change. Twenty dollars for some frozen milk and sugar, that was what he was thinking. The ingredients cost fourteen cents at most. Back at home a box of six costs two dollars. Et cetera. But I think we were all glad he finally caved in. It stopped Ryan from asking for it every ten minutes. And of course he needed more sugar, seeing that he still had two molars that weren't full of holes and was trying to complete the set. We all knew he wouldn't be throwing his ice cream to the birds.

We left the park after we finished our ice cream. As I got into the car, I eyed Ben sitting back there in the lap of luxury. Everyone except for Ryan and me was enjoying generous legroom: Mom and Dad were up front with their seats pushed as far back as possible, and Ben had the entire third seat to himself. But I would never ask to drive just to get a little extra legroom, not with the worst back-seat drivers known to man in the car. Those two had devised their own cockamamie set of traffic laws, and if you didn't know that you must decrease your speed to 23 MPH in the first ten minutes of a rainstorm, then you'd hear it. And if you did actually go 23 MPH the next time it rained, just so you wouldn't have to listen to them, the law would suddenly be amended to include having your windshield wipers on high (not medium), and by the way, the 23 MPH had been recently changed to 21 MPH, so no matter what you did you'd still have to suffer through a rambling lecture. No thank you. Besides, I figured it was better to get a few minutes of studying in. I took out my words.

"Seatbelts on?" Dad said.

Nobody answered him.

"Let's play twenty questions," Ryan said after a few minutes of blissful silence.

"Yeah," Ben said.

"Hannah?" Ryan said.

"No. I'm studying," I said.

"Come on, I'll pick something funny, Han. Just one game," Ryan said.

"All right, fine." Sometimes it was faster to just play a round than to argue with him. I turned to Ben. "You ask the first question."

"Is it termites?" Ben said.

"No, that's one," Ryan said.

"You want to ask bigger questions, Fuzz. Don't guess any specific things until you have more clues. Although, even I thought he might pick termites, so good job," I said. "OK, is it alive?"

"No, it's not alive. Well, I guess it—no, fine, it it's not alive. Two questions," Ryan said.

"Is it black?" Ben said.

"No. Three," Ryan said.

"Can it fit in the palm of your hand?" I said.

"Yes—what the? Why are we going here?" Ryan said.

"We're eating in tonight," Dad said. He had pulled into the parking lot of a supermarket.

"Why?" Ryan said.

"We'll go out tomorrow night. Everyone can pick what they want here," Dad said.

Doubtful. And it wasn't about spending the money, although Dad had already gotten feigning displeasure of Floridian prices down to a science. It was about accommodating Ben. He would nibble at restaurant chicken fingers, but devour his favorite frozen brand. No doubt they wanted to get a good meal into him.

I certainly didn't mind. The thought of eating something quick and then holing up in a corner somewhere was downright comforting to me. Or at least as comforting as I was going to get on this trip.

We entered our old stomping grounds and then split up to choose our dinners from the shelves. Mom and Dad selected some classics: a TV dinner for each of them as well as a jumbo can of Campbell's vegetable soup (undented) for everyone to share. Ben got his chicken fingers and juice boxes, and Ryan followed his lead and dined on chicken fingers as well (and somehow managed to get even more ice cream out of them). I just grabbed a sandwich from the deli.

When we returned to the hotel, Mom and Dad started heating up the food while we tried to find somewhere to sit, the lack of a kitchen table certainly not helping the situation. Ryan and Ben ended up kneeling next to the coffee table, while I sat on the couch and tried to balance my plate in my lap.

"What did everyone think of EPCOT?" Dad said. He and Mom were standing in the kitchen doorway eating their soup.

"There weren't any roller coasters there. They need to get with the times," Ryan said.

"The Maelstrom is like a roller coaster," Mom said.

"Not really. Just because something goes faster than two miles an hour doesn't make it a roller coaster. It's just another boat ride. But still, that was like the only good ride there," Ryan said.

"Don't say things like that in front of your brother," Dad said.

"Or me. You're ruining the magic," I said.

"Did you enjoy EPCOT, Ben?" Dad said.

Ben took his chicken finger and whizzed it above his head in a wide arc, as if he were performing an air show for us. He accompanied this with the sound you make when you whistle by inhaling.

Well, there was your answer.

"Did you like it?" Mom said.

"No bugs there," Ben said.

"That's quite an inscrutable observation," I said.

No. That wasn't the right word, was it? Did inscrutable mean profound and wise? Or was it sapient I was thinking of? Inscrutable meant—oh, as if they'd ever know the difference. Obfuscate. I speak SAT in front of my parents so I can obfuscate what I'm really saying.

"We're all going to die from high blood pressure," Ryan said.

"Why would you say something like that?" Dad said.

"This soup is full of salt, because salt preserves things. It'll give us high blood pressure. You can die from that, you know," Ryan said.

"Who told you this?" Dad said.

"Everybody knows it," Ryan said.

He was clever sometimes, that brother of mine. And he did have a good memory as well. Sad that it would probably all go to waste on French fry orders.

"What do you think this soup tastes like?" I said.

"Like soup. Eat it," Dad said.

"I think it lacks any real taste. If you took away the salt, you wouldn't taste anything," I said.

"Yeah, really. Salt and maybe an ounce of canned tomatoes. How can you eat it all the time, Dad?" Ryan said.

"I think it's fine," Dad said.

"You can't taste anything," Ryan said.

"That's enough," Mom said.

"Well, I'm done," I said. I retreated to the farthest corner I could find, although it really didn't matter where I sat—Ryan and Ben were kneeling in the middle of the tiny room, so there was no sanctuary to be found here. I took out my math book.

Today was Sunday. I just had to get through seven more. Six if I didn't count the flight home. Tomorrow they would be getting their tests back. I was pretty sure I had scored at least a ninety. Good enough for BC.

Seven

October

My back was killing me.

There were two beds in this so-called suite, and Mom and Dad obviously had one of them. So each night Ryan and I had been playing rock, paper, scissors for who would share the bed with Ben. I could usually beat him, because if it was a tie, he would always choose the opposite of the last throw. Without fail. But last night, he hadn't. He had finally learned, and I was stuck with the cot.

But the floor probably would have been preferable to this shoddy cot. All night it had felt as if someone had been jamming a rod against my back. Those rolled-up T-shirts I put under me were worthless. I tried not to think about it. I tried imagining I was on a king-size waterbed surrounded by soft pillows, but all I could feel was Mr. Rod. Moving onto my side didn't work, either. I was skinny, but not skinny enough to fit on half a cot. Maybe Ben could have, but I would have been kicked out of the family if I had suggested he switch with me. Sirens would go off, and men in white smocks would charge into the room and haul me away.

The only consolation to a stiff back and lack of sleep was that we were going to a water park today. It was the one and only planned activity that I had any interest in on this trip. I suspected that the only reason we were going was because of that enormous kiddie section I had seen Mom eyeing in her guidebook, but any reason was fine with me if it meant avoiding another day at the infantile Magic Kingdom.

Just to prove me right, Mom and Dad marched us right to the kiddie section the moment we arrived. We barely managed to stake out an umbrella and a few chairs without getting run down by the other crazed families. They were practically engaged in hand-to-hand combat over some chaise lounges.

"Everyone needs to reapply their sunscreen," Mom said, even though we had just put it on all of thirty minutes ago.

She slathered another half a bottle on poor Ben. I felt bad for him—she was too rough when she did it, as if she were trying to force the sunscreen into his pores. And she always put an excessive amount on. He looked like a greased cookie sheet afterward.

We had already changed into our bathing suits at the hotel, so we all just removed our outer layer of clothing. Seeing your parents in their bathing suits was one of those things that you should try to avoid in life if at all possible. It made you nervous that you were peering twenty years into the future. I would personally rather skip the preview and just deal with it when the time came. Mom's bathing suit had one of those little skirts that concealed her rear, even though she didn't really need it. Frankly, she would be doing us all a favor if she traded with some of the more scantily clad ladies here. Let's just say a skirt wouldn't hurt. Or even a long T-shirt. All the way to the knees, please. Dad wasn't doing much better, with his stomach and chest white enough to blind you and his salmon-armed farmer tan from wearing a T-shirt the past few days. Over here we had Ben in a lovely hand-me-down suit from Ryan. The pockets may have been worn, but not to worry. It was still bright orange! And too big for him. Last but not least, we were all streaked with white sunscreen, SPF 245. We were a sad looking lot.

Before Ryan and I could attempt our escape, Dad said we had to coordinate shifts for watching Ben. I almost expected him to start drawing up a schedule right there in the sand. I was surprised they were even going to let Ryan or me watch Ben. Sometimes there were surprisingly large holes in their overprotection—letting us watch Ben, or having Ryan sit alone on a bench as punishment. But then again there were lifeguards posted every ten feet here. Really, it was their dream environment. If they could move us to Kiddie Section, Typhoon Lagoon they would. Dad went to put our valuables in a locker, and then he and Mom took the first shift.

We had seen a wave pool when we first came in, so Ryan and I decided to check it out. Every few minutes a train whistle would sound, which meant a giant wave was coming. The crowd would let out a collective scream, and then there would be this tremendous whoosh, like the noise trap doors made in cartoons when they opened under people's feet. The screams would grow louder until the gigantic wave finally arrived and instantly silenced everyone. We attempted to swim out to the deep end, but the mob was so thick that we were only able to ride a couple of waves before Ryan had to go back and begin his shift. I went on a few water slides by myself, and then I headed back to the kiddie section when I felt like a half hour had passed. Ryan was sitting under the umbrella with his eyes closed, no doubt longing for a handheld video game.

"You're not even watching him," I said.

"I look over there every now and then. He's fine, nobody even needs to watch him." He stood up. "Oh, and let me give you Mom's very important instructions: Make him take a break every fifteen minutes so he doesn't get pruney."

"I'm not doing that."

"Obviously I didn't."

"Where are they?"

"At the lazy river. The most boring ride here, of course. They're coming back to relieve you in a half an hour."

"OK. When they get back we'll do speed slides."

I sat in the chair and took my list of words out. It was funny, how I was studying to get this formidable vocabulary while Ben probably didn't use more than a couple hundred words, if that. I knew perfidious and Ben knew yeah. Shelly's sister was a chatterbox, and she was only five. But then again, what word did she say that was so advanced? Cheerios? Maybe Ben was just quiet and internalizing it all. How did we know what he was thinking? There was nothing wrong with the silent type. Look at John Wayne or Charlie Chaplin.

I put my words down and looked over at him. He was standing under a six-foot-high mushroom, which had water spilling down its cap. Every twenty seconds or so, he would take a giant karate chop at the stream of water. Frankly, it didn't seem fair that he had to spend all day cloistered under some dull mushroom. Here we were surrounded by exciting water slides, and all Ben was doing was taking a long shower. I figured we could sneak off and be back before Mom and Dad returned, maybe try out that Storm Chaser ride I'd passed by earlier. How dangerous could it be if you were just sitting in a tube? And we had put all of our valuables in the lockers, so it really didn't matter if we left.

"Hey B, want to try a big kid ride? A tube ride?"

"Yeah!" He took one final chop at the water and then ran over to me.

We walked to the bottom of the Storm Chaser slide and waited for a tube, but a few of the riders wouldn't give theirs up because they said they were going on again. There always had to be some of those people everywhere you went. The same kind who would whiz past you in the breakdown lane during a traffic jam. You would have thought the lifeguard would force them to hand over their tubes and wait in line like everyone else, but she was clearly too concerned with her optimum tanning position. I had to admit it was pretty clever of Disney to force you to watch the riders grinning and cheering as they plummeted into the pool. It made you feel like you had to go on it, no matter how long the line was. Free advertising.

I finally got two tubes and handed one to Ben.

"So are you excited?" I said.

"Yeah yeah."

I smiled. The tube was as big as him.

But then I suddenly realized he might not be tall enough to go on the ride. All of the people coming down were teenagers or adults.

What if there was a height restriction?

We went and stood in another line. This one curved around some plastic rock formations, and we had a perfect vantage point of everybody waiting. And at least half of the kids in line were younger than Ben. It was hard sometimes not to let Mom and Dad's paranoia rub off on you. Who wouldn't be a little worried, with the way they overprotected him? The longer I looked at those kids in line, the more angry I grew with my parents for locking poor Ben up in that depressing kiddie area all day while all of the other kids with obsession-free parents were laughing it up on the real rides.

"You ready?" I said.

"How fast is it?"

"Not too fast. Don't be nervous. Look at all the kids here that are smaller than you. That kid's like two years old."

"I want real fast."

I smiled. He wasn't a baby like everyone thought.

"This is pretty fast," I said. "But there's one thing you have to remember to do for me. You have to hold the handles tight, like this."

I clenched the handles and leaned back onto the tube, looking up at the sky. I felt like Jesus on the big cross in church.

"I can hold on," Ben said.

"Let me see you do it."

He held the handles and leaned back, but of course he made a noise. It sounded like a seagull.

"Is that your holding-on noise?" I said.

"Yeah." Then he looked straight ahead and smiled. What a smile he had. Sly. A General George Washington on the dollar bill smile.

In about five minutes we had barely moved five feet. That was by far the most frustrating thing about Disney World. The . . .constant . . .waiting. Their little fastpass gimmick that was supposed to hold your place in line barely made a difference overall. On any remotely popular ride, you just needed to brace yourself for an endless wait as they weaved you in and out of a complex labyrinth of ropes. The annoying thing was, they were aware of how many people came to each park. They forced every single body through those turnstiles, excessive girth be damned. So why not use all of this data that they collected? Why not say, OK, five billion people attend this water park even in October when nobody is on school break, so let's try to add a few more rides or hire some more staff. God forbid capitalist Disney put up a sign warning anyone about how crowded the park was. Instead they just kept jamming patrons through the front gates 'til they couldn't jam no more. Nobody cared if you had to wait because guess what, you already paid your exorbitant, non-refundable admission. The joke was on you.

I stood on my tiptoes and saw that we had made decent progress in the line. I tried to decide whether I should go first or if Ben should. If I went first, I could be waiting at the bottom when he came out. But it was probably better if I was the one to come up behind him. Not to mention Fat Guy with Hairy Stomach was directly behind us in line. I couldn't let that creature crash into Ben. I would be the buffer at least.

"You go first, OK?" I said when it was almost our turn.

He nodded.

The lifeguard held out his arm, and the lady in front of us stood behind it.

"Here, put your tube behind you and grab the handles so you'll be ready to go," I said. "You excited?"

"Yes."

"Go," the lifeguard said in the most indifferent voice you'd ever heard.

The lady plunked down into her tube and then drifted down the slide a few seconds later.

I nudged Ben a little, and he went and stood behind the lifeguard's arm.

"Remember, hold those handles. You'll remember for me, right?" God, what if he let go? He might think it'd be funny to let go. He would flop all over the place and bang into the walls. His mouth would fill up with water and he'd choke. "Don't let go."

The lifeguard raised his arm as if it required an incredible amount of energy to do so. Ben took a running start and swung his tube out in front of him. He landed perfectly in the center of it and then disappeared down the slide.

"Hey, no running!" the lifeguard said, jumping from his seat.

I stared at the spot where I had last seen Ben in disbelief. My little brother—who would still be bathing in Kiddie Land if it were up to my parents—had just looked like a professional water-slide rider.

The lifeguard saw me grinning. I pressed my lips together and tried to look serious.

"You aren't supposed to run," he said loudly.

That certainly woke him up. He was about to slip into a coma until Ben's turn.

"I'll tell him. I promise."

"You can go ahead." He didn't even bother putting out his arm.

I stepped very gingerly into my tube and floated down the slide. As soon as I was out of Coma's sight, I tried to catch up to Ben by propelling myself down the slide with my hands and feet. About twenty seconds later, I heard a gut-wrenching scream that sounded exactly like him. The sort of scream someone might make if they had gone over the side of this very slide and was now plummeting to the ground.

But then all of a sudden he made his famous motorcycle noise. I was so relieved to hear that sound that I wanted to repeat it back to him, like an intricate bird call. And of course I felt foolish for overreacting. I should have known he would be fine. He loved being in our pool back at home. If Ben could swim instead of walk his way through life, he would.

Shortly after he made the motorcycle noise, my tube whizzed around a sharp bend and hurled me directly into a tunnel. Everything grew pitch black for a few moments before I was thrown back into the light. It was exhilarating, and certainly deserving of a motorcycle noise. When I splashed down into the pool, he was waiting for me at the bottom of the steps, the water all the way up to his chest.

"Again."

"OK. You liked it?"

"Yeah." He nodded vigorously.

Ben and I officially joined the Jerk Club and kept our tubes. We got back in line behind this guy and girl who were about my age. Whenever the guy went to talk to the girl, he would lean in unnecessarily close and give her this long, exaggerated look. He kept up this little act, using the same lean and sappy gaze move, as if it was some sort of novel approach that had never been tried on a girl before. Of course I knew it was impolite for me to stare. But I was seriously on the verge of yelling come on, buddy, do us all a favor and just kiss her already. You better hurry up before Mommy and Daddy come back to get you.

When we were about halfway through the line, he finally leaned in all the way, and they started to kiss.

"Kkkkwwwwwooooossshhh," Ben said loudly.

The guy stopped and looked at us, and then the girl turned around too. I started to pick at a bit of loose rock on the wall, and they eventually returned to their gazefest and forgot about us.

To be honest, there were times when I really did wish I had a boyfriend. Skipping all of the school dances because you didn't want to lurk in the corner with your friend pretending not to notice the swarm of couples before you did hit a nerve sometimes. It made me tempted to just walk up to Kyle Reid and say, I know my family is crazy, and I know I'm an inexperienced sixteen-year-old who has never had a boyfriend, but I also know you like me, so maybe we could at least give it a shot. I mean, I probably was a little bit jealous. Not of this girl in particular, since her boyfriend looked like he could have been Lassie the Dog's stunt double. But they did remind me of what I was missing, and what I would be missing for a while.

My one and only experience in this area was Rob O'Donnell, who came up to me while I was getting a soda at Sarah Johnson's birthday party and just started kissing me out of the blue. I played it off like it was nothing extraordinary but rather something I'd been expecting, even though it was my first kiss. I think I did a decent job, all things considered. The way he strutted back to his group of friends made me realize it was entirely possible that I had only been kissed because of some dare. Fine with me though—my initial reaction was pure relief. At least now when I went to college, I wouldn't have to lie about it. Not having a boyfriend seemed much more forgivable than never having been kissed.

When we finally got to the front of the line, the lifeguard eyed Ben.

"Walk slowly this time."

"He knows, I told him," I said. "Slow into the tube, Ben, OK? No running or jumping."

I had really forgotten to tell him. It was thanks to those two lovebirds sucking face—they had distracted me. Frankly, I was surprised Coma even remembered us. We couldn't have been the only delinquents in line. Ben's bright orange shorts had to be the reason. Everybody else was wearing fancy bathing suits with little horses sewn onto them. No doubt they weren't staying at the Econo Suites with the unidentifiable smells or the one kitchen cabinet that refused to close unless you tied its handle to the one next to it with some dental floss so you wouldn't keep hitting your knees on it. And the comfortable cots.

I didn't hear Ben scream this time. He was at the top of stairs when I splashed into the pool.

"Again," he said.

"I think we better go check in. Then we'll do more." I had a feeling we had already been gone for a half an hour. Which was why Dad's system was stupid—there were no clocks here, so how could you really know how much time had gone by? Time passed differently at a water park than, say, during math class.

We gave up our tubes and then walked toward our umbrella. As we got closer, I thought I heard Mom say there they are. Ryan was with them, and they were all staring at us.

I put my hand on Ben's back, but he shook it off.

"Hi," I said.

"Where were you?" Dad said.

"I took Ben on a ride."

"You were supposed to stay here," Dad said.

"What ride?" Mom said at the same time.

"A tube ride."

"You did? Which one?" Ryan said.

"Who told you to take him on a ride? You were supposed to stay right here," Dad said.

"Calm down. It was just a safe little tube ride. Come on, Ryan. Let's take him on some others."

"OK, let's go," Ryan said.

"Not so fast. You aren't going any—" Dad said.

"The line was full of kids half his size, Dad. Who would want to sit in this kiddie pond all day? Let's go Ryan," I said.

"Hannah, stop being cute," Dad said. Then he pointed his darn index finger at the sky. "There's another issue here. No one was watching our belongings."

"There's nothing here worth more than two dollars," I said.

"Your chemistry book is here," Dad said.

"Dad, who's going to steal a chemistry book at a water park?" Ryan said.

"Seriously, I'm sure they'd love the bonus SAT words they'd get with it. What a score that would be," I said.

"Please—" Mom said.

"Can Hannah take me on the rides?" Ben said.

Everyone turned and looked at him with surprise, as if we had forgotten he was even there, never mind the subject of the discussion. Then I looked over at my parents, who exchanged strange little glances with each other.

"All right, you and Ryan take him with you, but let's all come back here in about an hour to check in. And stay together," Dad said.

"She's not in trouble?" Ryan said.

"Let's go," I said, grabbing Ryan's arm.

"Wait, let me put some more sunscreen on Ben," Mom said.

"He's fine," I said over my shoulder.

The three of us walked to the slide in silence. It took me a few minutes to realize why my parents had looked at each other that way. That was the first time Ben had ever really asked for anything. Granted, he would ask for things in a roundabout, nonchalant way, like saying "again" when he wanted another turn on the ride. But he would never just come right out and beg for cookies or demand to stay up late. Which was shocking, when you thought about it, because that was all kids ever did. But not Ben. It was like the only punctuation mark he was aware of was the period. And if he didn't want to do something, if he didn't want to eat Aunt Lydia's potatoes, he wouldn't ask for chicken nuggets instead. He simply wouldn't eat them.

I was pretty pleased with myself, frankly. For once, I had forced my parents to let Ben do something he actually wanted to do. I knew I wasn't saving the world here—or even saving Ben with such a small gesture. When I went away to college, there would be no one to intervene when he was inevitably put back under another mushroom. But it felt good all the same.

\#

This trip was wearing on us. My back was killing me yet again because I had somehow devolved into the world's worst rock, paper, scissors player. We all kept bumping into each other in our matchbox of a hotel room. I had sunburn. Everywhere. Ryan was even more whiny and fidgety than usual. Ben was just sitting on the floor ignoring everyone. Mom and Dad wouldn't tell us where we were going. They'd made peanut butter and jelly sandwiches again. Oh, and Aunt Flo had decided to come visit me two days early. It was a delightful morning.

"This hotel sucks," Ryan said to me.

I didn't look up from my list of words. He was right of course, but what good did it do complaining about it? It certainly wasn't going to turn my cot into a feather bed.

"Please keep your voice down. Your mother is having one of her headaches today," Dad said. He pointed at the bathroom door.

She was always having one or some or all of her headaches lately, in case he hadn't noticed.

"I wasn't yelling," Ryan said.

"I don't want to hear that talk. And I especially don't want to hear it in front of your mother. You don't know how much work—" Dad said.

"Jeez, calm down. This room is fine for five people."

"You don't understand what's involved in planning these vacations for you."

"You got it through a travel agency, I thought. They did it all for you."

"Ryan, please don't comment on things you don't understand."

Well, I understood, even if I wasn't commenting. Mom and Dad loved that we were all jammed into one room because it meant that Ben would be on everyone's radar at all times. If he tried to sleepwalk, we'd all know. He'd have to climb over me and my cot to get by. I also happened to know that was why his bedroom back home was in the corner of the house, right next to their room. They had probably learned to sleep with their eyes open so they could watch if he walked past.

There was a large brochure display in the hotel lobby, and on the walk to the car Ryan showed me two he had picked up: one for Uncle Joe's Alligator Farm, which had a picture of two scrawny gators who looked to be about three hundred years old on the cover, and another featuring a chair made out of iron spikes. A torture museum. It didn't surprise me that it would appeal to a fourteen-year-old boy, but the truth was I also found it fascinating in a morbid sort of way. The Holocaust, serial killers, Genghis Khan—all of it interested me. Man had devised so many ways to be cruel and awful to others, and if you were just going about your day it was easy to forget that. Disney World was set up to purposely make you forget it, in fact. I went back and forth about how I really felt toward humanity and the whole are humans innately good or evil question.

I pointed to the spiked chair. "I'd go there. But they wouldn't even let Ben see the cover of that brochure."

"There's more than one kid in this family," Ryan said.

I actually felt bad for Ryan then. He was really your classic middle child, starved for attention, and that never led to anything good when it came to teenage boys.

When everyone was in the car, Ryan held the brochure in the air.

"I found a great thing to do today. Let's go to this torture museum."

"That's horrible," Mom said.

"No," Dad said.

"I'll go there," I said.

"I think it looks interesting." Ryan shoved the brochure toward them. "You shouldn't ignore history."

"That's enough, we're not going there. Ben would be frightened," Dad said.

"Well if we can't go to the torture museum, then what are we doing?" Ryan said.

"Magic kingdom," Mom said.

"Again?" I said. It came out as a kind of half-complaint, as if I had tried to make it sound like a question but couldn't hide my annoyance.

"We didn't finish all the rides. There are more for Ben that we didn't do," Dad said.

I looked back at him. He was trying to squish He-Man's head into the ashtray, oblivious to all of this. I had a feeling we could be on our way to the town dump and it'd be the same to him.

The only ride that I had any interest in at the Magic Kingdom was Space Mountain. It was my white whale. On our last vacation I was declared too young to ride it alone, and on Saturday I had been too wrapped up in my SAT words to give it much thought. But what I wanted more than a ride on some roller coaster was a break from everyone—somewhere other than the bathroom where I could be alone with my thoughts for five minutes. When else in life were you forced to spend every waking and sleeping moment with other people? They called this a vacation? Instead it was bringing out the worst in us. Even I was getting pulled into family dramas that I was normally so good at staying out of.

"Why can't we go somewhere else today?" Ryan said.

"No complaining please," Dad said in this strange, sing-song voice. You had to wonder if he was losing it a bit as well.

"Let's go to Typhoon Lagoon again," Ryan said.

"We were just there yesterday," Mom said.

"We were just at Magic Kingdom Saturday," Ryan said.

"I'll go to Typhoon Lagoon," I said.

"Your mother took the time to plan this day, and you are going to do what she decided. It's ungrateful of you to keep questioning her plans," Dad said.

"OK. God," Ryan said.

I'd always found it somewhat creepy how he would say sentences like that right in front of her. He treated her like a fragile infant sometimes, always rushing to her defense. She wasn't the strongest person I knew by any means, but she wasn't that much of a weakling, either.

"Tomorrow I thought we'd have breakfast out," Mom said.

It was about time. Honest to God I couldn't eat another bowl of Rice Krispies if my life depended on it. One more spoonful and we were all going to turn into the Snap, Crackle, Pop guys on the box.

"Good. Where?" I said.

"At the Crystal Palace with the Disney characters," Mom said.

"Oh no," Ryan said, while I closed my eyes slowly and tried to pretend that I was somewhere else. It wasn't working.

"But it's supposed to have a really nice buffet," Mom said.

"I'm sorry, but sixteen-year-olds don't eat breakfast with Disney characters," I said.

"And Ben doesn't even want to go. It's for babies," Ryan said.

"You two are prejudicing Ben from not going," Dad said, taking much longer than usual to chime in. He probably didn't want to go either.

"Like Ben would even like it. Those characters are so corny. They do the exact same tricks to every table. Pluto always steals your hat," Ryan said.

I laughed. "Oh yeah, and then he does that sad little act of looking around for it, like he doesn't know where it is. You remember everything, Sparks."

"Sparks," Ben said.

"Fine, we won't go," Mom said.

"No Sue, we can go. I'm sure Ben will enjoy it. I'm sure everyone will," Dad said.

"No, that's all right. We'll go somewhere else," Mom said.

Nobody said anything. Part of me wanted to believe this was the second victory in the fight for Ben's freedom. But something told me that Pluto would be stealing Fuzzhead's hat tomorrow morning.

After we parked our car, we still had to walk approximately two miles to the tram stop. I found it incredible that so many people wanted to patronize this place that it required a tram to haul them all to the front gate. It boggled the mind, really. Rows upon rows of cars. Old jalopies and gigantic SUVs waiting patiently for their owners in the blazing Floridian sun. Why couldn't all of this energy and determination be harnessed for some sort of useful purpose?

"Sue, let me take that for you. Kids, why is your mother carrying two bags while none of you are carrying any?" Dad said.

"Because they're her bags," Ryan said.

"Exactly," I said quietly.

"That one is the lunch bag," Mom said, pointing to the diaper bag in Dad's hand. As if any of us needed help identifying that one.

"Why do we bring a diaper bag when the youngest person here is eight? It makes us look even more suspicious," I said.

"We're just lucky they don't check it. Think of how much money we are saving," Dad said.

"How about I throw that bag away and buy us all hamburgers?" Ryan said.

"No way," Ben said.

"Chicken nuggets for you. Or maybe a nice juicy pizza?" Ryan said.

"That's enough," Dad said. He handed Ryan the diaper bag.

He thrust it into my arms. "Here. You're the oldest."

I swung it over my shoulder without saying anything, passive resistance style. I would carry ten diaper bags if it meant getting to the end of this trip. I even looked at Ryan with a half-smile, as if to say, this is how you do it my friend. Zen. Patience. Control.

"It's not vacation if you don't get to eat at restaurants," Ryan said, clearly ignoring the wisdom that my extra one year and three months brought me.

When we got inside the park, Dad stopped and turned around.

"Why don't we all try the Pirates of the Caribbean ride?" he said.

"Yeah," Ben said. He nodded so fast that his fuzzball jumped up and down.

Well, of course he was going to love the pirate ride. That was surprisingly clever of Dad. He had probably been keeping that one tucked away in his pocket so he could surprise Ben with it and look like the hero.

"Do you think he might get scared?" Mom said, without bothering to whisper.

"No, I think he'll like it," Dad said.

I could remember two things from the last trip that I liked about that ride. First, it was dark and cool in there and smelled pleasantly musty, like our shed. And second, your boat would dip down a slight hill when the ride started. Certainly not a roller coaster by any stretch of the imagination, but probably the closest I was going to get to raising my blood pressure above extremely bored.

When the ride was over, we were dumped into the gift shop, which contained every sort of pirate souvenir known to man. Ben made a beeline for the rifles and picked one up. He made his gun noise and then pulled the trigger, and the rifle grunted out a sad little explosion that wasn't half as good as his version. During the entire time we were in the gift shop, Mom trailed Ben and took approximately two hundred pictures of him. She probably realized that this was the happiest she was going to capture him looking.

After the pirates, Dad led us to the It's a Small World ride, located in Fantasyland. (And why, exactly, did that particular quadrant need its own special designation? As if the rest of this place was so grounded in reality.) We were all occupying ourselves by either standing there waiting patiently (Mom and Dad), reading our SAT words (me), or touching every inch of the dirty handrail (Ryan, according to Dad), when all of a sudden Ben thrust his hand toward the crowd and imitated a strong gust of wind. The noise grew louder and higher-pitched until he finally let forth a remarkably accurate rendition of an explosion. It had been quiet in line, since everyone was just waiting silently to find out how small our world really was, that Ben's pretend grenade might as well have been real, that was how obvious it was. Everyone within a mile radius turned to stare at us. You couldn't blame his militaristic mood, though. As soon as that pirate ride started, you found yourself on the High Seas, bombarded by cannonballs, threatened by surly men with swords. So it was Disney's fault, really. Ben was just following their lead.

Clearly my water slide lesson from yesterday had already been forgotten. Here we were waiting to go on yet another dumbed-down kiddie ride for Ben's sake. If my parents had any sort of relationship with reality they would see that all he really wanted to do was pirates at the Magic Kingdom, water slides at Typhoon Lagoon, and dinosaurs at EPCOT. The rest was just pointless to him.

"Hey He-man, you don't really want to go on this, do you?" I said when I was sure he was done launching grenades.

"Yeah it's for babies, right Ben?" Ryan said.

"Hannah, please stop trying to influence and prejudice him against what we've planned. You know he listens to everything you say," Dad said.

"He doesn't like to go on baby rides or stay in kiddie pools," I said.

"Well, I want to go on Small World. In fact I can hardly wait, I'm so excited. So you're all going on it for me," Dad said.

Ben laughed.

Dad had won again.

We played yet another round of How Many in Your Party, but I didn't even fight for Ben to sit with us. The operator put Ryan and me in the front row and Dad, Mom, and Ben behind us. Then we started to move even slower than Dad's driving past some cheaply made puppets. They kept blasting us with God-awful music that sounded like the *Chipmunks Christmas Album*, as if their singular goal was to get the song stuck in everyone's heads for the next three days. What was it with Disney and their obsession with pelting you with obnoxious music or commentary every minute? I think they wanted to make it impossible for you to sit back and relax or—God forbid—be with your own thoughts. A few minutes later, our boat dragged itself into a new room with more puppets and music. I took out my list of words, but Ryan nudged me.

"Hey, that one looks just like Dad," he said really loudly.

He pointed at a puppet right in front of our boat. It had a giant, circular head and a few thin lines of black hair, and it kept opening and closing its mouth as if it was badly lip-synching to the music. And it looked Asian. My parents liked to say Oriental, even though I had informed them more than once that it should only be used for rugs and soup. Although it wasn't like there were that many opportunities to offend in Whitetown, other than, say, when ordering Chinese takeout.

I spat my gum directly into the murky water, and Ben stood up and pointed at the puppet.

"Dad, Dad," he said. "What's for dinner, Dad?"

Then Ben did his vroom-vroom noise, which surprised me because he normally reserved it for fast-moving vehicles, and someone in a wheelchair could have beaten us in this watercraft. By now Ryan and I were in hysterics because Ben wouldn't stop turning around and yelling Dad, Dad at the puppet. And we were able to see the darn thing for about an hour since we were crawling along here. Then I happened to look over at Dad. His mouth was closed so tightly that his lips formed one straight line. It was pretty obvious that his feelings had been hurt (it was not the most flattering comparison), and I kind of felt bad for him. But even after seeing Dad pout, I still couldn't stop laughing. And I knew it wasn't even that funny. Maybe the grenade incident had primed us for laughter. Or maybe us kids just needed a release, and laughter was the closest thing at hand.

Ryan and I finally calmed down, but Mom was still trying to deal with Ben. She had at least gotten him to sit back down, but he was still yelling Dad, Dad, vroom, vroom at the puppet.

"Look what you've started, Ryan," Mom said.

"That's it, you're sitting on a bench for the next two rides. You always have to encourage them, don't you?" Dad said.

"I was just kidding around. Why can't we ever have a little fun?" Ryan said.

"Ryan—" Dad said.

"No, really. It's like you're both allergic to fun. This is a vacation, not a jail," Ryan said.

"Just turn around. Keep this up and watch where it leads you," Dad said.

Ryan finally stopped arguing and turned back around. But then a few moments later, he happened to look over at me. I saw that famous spark in his eyes, and before I even knew what I was doing, I imitated that puppet, crinkling my eyes and opening and closing my mouth in a mechanical way along with the music.

We both lost it. I fell over onto the side of the boat I was laughing so hard.

Ben stood up and leaned toward us. "What? What?"

Mom pulled him back down.

I saw Ryan pinch the top of his thigh to stop himself from laughing, and then he turned around to face Dad.

"OK, OK. I'm sorry. I'll be good," he said. Then he looked out the other side of the boat, keeping me totally out of his sight.

I had to admit for a minute there it did feel like old times, back when we rarely fought with each other and were more like allies against our parents. Before I even knew what an SAT test was, or when I thought I was going to live in North Prospect forever. A simpler time. I almost wanted to reach over and put my arm around old Sparks—-something I never did. I saw that this moment was the end of something. It was our final goof-off session, and I knew this because I was going to be the one to end them, and the arm around the shoulder would show him: no hard feelings, kid. Nothing lasts forever.

Instead I just lightly patted the top of his knee twice.

Then, still feeling warm and sentimental, I looked back at Ben. He had calmed down and was now sandwiched between his overprotective parents, off in his own world again—where you could be sure there weren't any singing puppets. He was probably daydreaming about termites. He looked so innocent, and it seemed appropriate that we were in a boat while I was feeling this way, because I was imagining grabbing a spare one and springing Ben and me out of here. Somehow making it to the ocean. Or at least a river—the ol' Mississip. We could float along on our merry way.

But that little daydream soon subsided, and it felt appropriate to leave it in Fantasyland.

When we got off the ride, Dad made sure the whole family was gathered around before addressing Ryan.

"For your punishment, you are sitting out the next three rides."

"Fine," Ryan said.

"And you're skipping dessert."

I shook my head in sympathy. He had to go for the jugular, didn't he?

We did a few more rides while Ryan sat on his bench, and I didn't even bring up riding my white whale. Instead I surreptitiously waved goodbye as we walked past it, because I was in closure mode. I doubted that I would ever see that ride again.

#

That night, we all put on the one nice outfit that Mom had made us bring because we were finally going out for a decent meal. She had called months in advance and made reservations to eat at the restaurant inside the castle. As soon as we sat down, the waiters started calling us Your Highness, Prince, and Princess. Your Highness, would you like more chocolate milk? I think I was willing to let most of the silliness slide because I knew I was going to get some real food out of this charade. We had a great view of the whole park, and everything was sparkling and lit up, so it did feel pretty romantic. There were even a few honeymoon-types fawning all over each other—although why anyone would pick this for their honeymoon spot over Hawaii was beyond me.

"Hey, how did you guys meet?" I said.

"What?" Dad said, squirming in his seat. Mom didn't take her eyes off the cup of coffee the waiter was filling.

You would have thought that I'd asked them to explain the mechanics of sex, with sock puppets please. While everyone else in the room was head over heels, they wouldn't even tell their own children how they met. If you added up the few snippets of the story that I had heard over the years, I probably knew five minutes worth, if that.

"How did you propose to Mom? Wasn't there some boat involved?" I said.

"There was a boat," Mom said.

"And?" I said.

"I proposed to her on a boat," Dad said.

"And you gave her that rock," Ryan said.

He nodded, and then the waiter arrived with our food and that was that.

About halfway through my dinner, I took a break from eating. I'd always found that if I just sat there and waited for a full minute or two, I could create more room in my stomach and then be able resume eating again. I never had to do the trick for dessert, of course.

"Hey Fuzz, did you see they're eating green Jello over there?" I said.

But he didn't seem to hear me. His eyes had grown soft and lazy, as if they were resting on a pillow, and he was gazing out into space.

I had seen him fall into a trance like this a handful of times, and it was truly frightening. You couldn't snap him out of it by talking to him or tapping him on the shoulder—he seemed completely unaware of where he was or who he was with. I couldn't remember the last time he had gone into one of his trances, so it seemed pretty obvious that this delightful trip was the cause of it. Not to mention he had been making more noises than ever this past week. It had practically become his primary means of communication. Noises as a first language.

I looked around to see if anyone else in the family had noticed, but of course they were all completely oblivious. I started working on my half-eaten baked potato while still keeping him in my sight. I'd eaten everything but the skin by the time he finally left his trance.

When the bill came, Dad placed his credit card on the little tray. If my father actually swore, he'd be cursing like a sailor right about now. Not because of the bill, even though the food was pricey— definitely more than Ponderosa's all-you-can-eat-for-7.99 special. It was because he refused to use a credit card unless it was absolutely necessary. Mom too, although I suspected she was just following his lead. They were so behind the times. Dad's card was untouched, as shiny as a bald guy's head. He was the only person of his generation who still wrote checks. At the grocery store he would neatly tear off the check and then step to the end of the register, always in everyone's way, to fill out his perfectly balanced checkbook while our ice cream melted and half the store stared as if witnessing some colonial re-enactment.

When we got back to the hotel, I retreated to the corner with my words. Ryan asked Ben if he wanted to go swimming in the pool, and Ben immediately ran and put on his florescent bathing suit.

"Hannah, come swimming with us," Ryan said.

"No thanks," I said.

"Come on, we need you for Marco Polo. Leave your stupid words for once. It won't *demolish* your chances of getting a perfect score."

I raised my eyebrows at him. It was a sad day when the biggest word you could think of was demolish.

"It's not very warm out at night," I said.

"So, it's heated. Come on," Ryan said.

I finally looked up from my list.

"Think about what you're swimming in. Do you really think the Econo Suites cleans their pool regularly? Why would a cheapo hotel like this take the time to flush out all of the little kid urine in there? If an animal stumbled into the pool one night and drowned, do you think they would make sure the water was safe for swimming? Or would they just scoop out the carcass and let you swim right away. Who's keeping tabs on them?" I said.

"Hannah, cut it out," Dad said.

But Ben and Ryan were just staring at me. They had already gone for a swim in there on Sunday. I looked over at poor Ben, wearing nothing but that orange bathing suit, his thin legs sticking out like those flamingos we had seen today.

"I don't want to go in anymore, do you?" Ryan said.

Ben shook his head.

"Don't listen to your sister. It's fine to go in," Mom said.

"Uh-uh. She's right. They probably hire some ex-con with stringy hair who's supposed to clean the filters and add the chlorine, and instead he just chain-smokes all day and tosses his cigarettes butts into the pool. I'm never going in that dead-possum-and-piss water again," Ryan said.

"Just look at the kitchen cabinet. Or the bathroom. If they can't properly care for a six-foot tub, what makes you think they're going to look after that comparatively gargantuan pool?" I said.

"Hannah, that's enough," Mom said.

"Oh, I'm so grossed out. There were like two hundred kids in the pool Sunday night. I bet they all peed in there," Ryan said.

"Eeeww," Ben said. He started laughing.

Sad, that I had to resort to this. But the horrified look on Ryan's face was worth it, frankly. It was the most entertained I'd been all day. Goodbye Fantasyland, we're in Hannahworld now.

Dad didn't say anything, but you could tell I had gotten to him—this was a man who cleaned our toothbrushes in the dishwasher, for God's sake. He knew that I was knowledgeable about things in life. For example, on another urine-related note, I had enlightened him about orange juice from concentrate, how it contained pee from the workers who were too lazy to go to the bathroom, so they just used the slabs of frozen OJ as their personal urinal. And how the U.S. Government actually allowed a certain percentage of urine in there. So Dad obviously agreed with me—he just didn't want to admit that I was right. He wanted to be the one and only sanitary authority in the family.

"Let's go to the arcade then. I have some quarters," Ryan said.

"Yeah," Ben said.

"Have fun," I said.

"Come on, Hannah," Ryan said.

"No, I'm studying."

"Please?"

"No."

"Put it down for ten minutes." He yanked the list from my hands. "You have to study every second of your vacation? You're annoying the hell out of me with this."

"Give it back."

"No. Come to the arcade."

"Cut it out, you two," Dad said.

"Ryan, I'm not kidding," I said.

"Just because you're older doesn't make you God, some God who can't even go to the arcade for ten minutes with her only two brothers."

"Would you please just let me study my goddamn SAT words

so I can get into college and the hell out of North Prospect."

"Well, fine. Our little Einstein needs to study. I'd love it if you got into the University of Antarctica. I'd help you get in today if I could." Ryan threw the list at me.

"I have a question for you, Ryan. Where's your homework? You're telling me you don't have any, even though you took a whole week off from your sophomore year? I find that incredible, really."

"Shut up." He glanced at Mom. She and Dad both looked like they wanted to weigh in but were a little too taken aback by our fighting to actually interfere.

"You know, you're a fool if you think you have a future in North Prospect. Let me tell you something. If you don't go to college, you're going to end up working as either a burger flipper, a shelf stocker, or a pot dealer."

"Hannah, what a terrible—" Mom said.

"Not that you'd learn education is important in this house," I said.

"That's not true," Dad said.

"I don't want to talk about this anymore. I just want to study. That's all I've wanted to do from the beginning. But have I complained? No. I've gone on your stupid rides, and eaten your soggy peanut butter and jelly sandwiches, and stayed in your cramped hotel room. Now I just want to be left alone." I looked at Ryan. "And don't ever say you weren't warned. Because I just told you the truth."

Good Lord. Ryan was turning into a high school dropout. Ben was turning into Charlie Chaplin. I was turning into some pissy teenage girl who couldn't control her emotions.

This trip was turning into a complete nightmare.

Eight

October

The whole idea of standing in line in the blazing Floridian sun to meet some guy dressed up as a giant cloth duck seemed ridiculous to me. And to top it off, Disney didn't let these characters say a peep to their fans. Not one word. Because God forbid they pay their costume wearers more than minimum wage and find someone who actually could converse. All of these poor kids probably watched countless hours of cartoons in preparation for their big trip, only to come here and discover that all of their friends were mutes.

Now we were finally getting to meet the elusive Mickey Mouse. It had only taken us six days. He owned the place, so apparently that meant he had to clock in a whopping five minutes of face time a week. Again, way to think of the kids. You make him the star of all the advertisements, get the poor kids thinking they were going to see him as soon as they set foot in the place, and then never have him show up. But they gave you plenty of the two-bit characters, like the villain from *Robin Hood*. Mickey was dressed up in a spacesuit, presumably so we wouldn't forget that we were in EPCOT. For the second time. Even Ben, who was more interested in flies on the Monorail window than in any of the other characters, wanted to shake his hand. Pretty impressive, Disney.

But I didn't care that we were at EPCOT again, waiting in line to see a stuffed mouse. After last night's outburst, I had promised myself I would revert back to passive resistance mode. I needed to get re-grounded, because that embarrassing display of emotion was not me. I was so tantalizingly close to the end of this trip. I just had to stay focused. Focused and grounded.

There were nearly as many people in line to see Mickey as there had been for my white whale. Most of the kids were smiling, but a few of them were bawling. Clearly these kids were being forced by their parents to stand there and talk to the scary, unnaturally large mouse. Stop crying, Donnie. This will be fun. Look, there he is. There's Mickey Mouse. Waahhh! Poor kids.

A little boy in front of us was clutching an autograph book and an oversized pencil with a maroon tassel hanging from the eraser. He was beaming, his smile so wide it was spilling over the side of his cheeks. When it was almost his turn, he started bouncing up and down. As I watched him bounce and tap his feet and wiggle his little fingers, I tried to remember the last time I had been that full of pure joy and excitement. Or when Ryan had been, or my parents. Or anyone over ten years old. What happened to us when we grew up? All it took for this little boy was some stranger in a costume signing a fictional character's name.

I looked over at Ryan, who was proving my point quite nicely. He looked like he might try to take that tasseled pencil from the boy and stab Mickey with it. Unlike me, he had not bounced back from our little spat last night.

When it was our turn, our parents crept toward us, Mom armed with her camera. Ben walked right up to Mickey and commenced staring at his big shoes. Then Mickey tried to put his hand on Ben's shoulder, but Ben dodged it by moving about six inches to the left. Frankly I was glad. I would have been offended if he had let Mickey do it and not me.

When Mom finished taking her seventeen thousandth picture, Ryan approached Mickey.

"Hey Mickey, can I ask you a few questions?" he said.

Mickey nodded.

"Do you live in that big castle over there?"

He nodded vigorously.

"Do you hang out with Goofy a lot?"

More nodding.

"Did you ever get to second base with Minnie?"

Mickey immediately covered his mouth, as if he was extremely shocked and embarrassed. Ben started to laugh even though he couldn't have possibly known what Ryan was referring to. Even I was smiling. After all, it was a pretty good reaction on Mickey's part. It was probably some skinny gay guy in there, bored out of his mind, and now at least he had a decent story to tell when all the characters went to the bar after work. Or maybe they prepared them in their character training for all of the wise-ass kids they'd have to deal with. Now what about sexual jokes regarding Minnie, class? Charles? Hand over mouth, sir! Yes, that's the one, good work Charles.

Dad was starting to get riled up, like a dog that suspected you were taking him some place bad, most likely the vet, but wasn't exactly sure where. He came over to us.

"Thanks Mickey," Dad said. He nodded toward where Mom was standing to move us along.

"Yeah, thanks a bunch, Mickey," Ryan said.

Mickey gave us a deflated wave.

"What did you say to him, Ryan?" Dad said when we were out of Mickey's hearing range.

"Nothing. I asked him if he lived in the castle and all."

"Ben, what did he ask him about?" Dad said.

"Oh, come on," Ryan said.

"Baseball," Ben said.

Ryan and I laughed.

Mom then decided that we should walk to the Universe of Energy to do a final encore of the only ride in EPCOT that Ben had shown any interest in: the dinosaurs. After the dinosaurs, we went on a few more unmemorable rides and then walked seventeen miles to the American Pavilion, where Dad bought us hamburgers for lunch. Ryan took about two bites of his and then pushed it away, pressing his finger deep into the bun. The poor kid had been fighting for a burger for so long that when he finally got to eat one, he had no desire to. It was classic John and Sue Sampson. They probably knew the whole time that they were going to buy us hamburgers, but they figured they'd save it until the end, as a treat. But at this point, we were so worn down by long lines, boring rides, and crammed quarters that even the juiciest hamburger we'd ever tasted (and surely this was not it) wouldn't have fazed us. Even I, the oldest and most patient, just wanted to go home and forget this terrible trip.

After the anticlimactic hamburgers, we started the long walk back toward all of the rides. I suddenly realized that I could hear some sort of humming in the background. It sounded like the filter on the fish tank we used to have until the heater malfunctioned and cooked the unlucky guppies to death. I looked over at Ben. He was moving his arms back and forth like a cross-country skier, and emitting these manic little hums. Good Lord. Just in case there was any doubt that things were getting worse with him, here was another sign—first the trance, and now maniacal humming. And everyone else was oblivious to what was happening to him, too busy fiddling with their cameras or pouting incessantly or calculating how much tonight's dinner was going to cost. Per person.

"Hey Fuzzy Wuzzy, remember when you were the first person to find that termite? Where was it again?" I said.

"Kitchen window!"

Well, at least he could still talk.

I turned around and looked at my Parents in Denial. Dad had unfolded his map and was now tracing his finger over it.

"Where are we going? We've done every single ride here," Ryan said.

"Spaceship Earth?" Mom said.

"Sure," Dad said. He turned the map sideways and started tracing another path with his finger, mouthing some words to himself.

"We've already done that. I'm not going in that golf ball again,"

Ryan said.

"Yes you—" Mom said.

"No," Dad said. "You know what? That's fine. He doesn't have to sit through it if it's such agony for him. Every time we go on a ride from now on, he can just find a bench and wait for us there. Don't worry, we won't make you suffer through another one."

"Thank God," Ryan said.

"And since we paid your admission fee, we'll just take it out of your bank account," Dad said.

"Well, at least give me three dollars credit for sitting through that last one," Ryan said.

Dad paused, and it seemed like the part of him with the occasional, decent sense of humor just wanted to stop being the dad for a moment and have a good laugh at that. Clearly he could have used one.

"You have a terrible chip on your shoulder," Mom said.

"It's unfair how I'm always getting yelled at. That's your only interaction with me lately. Yelling," Ryan said.

"That's because you —" Dad said.

I sped up to get away from the pointless, circular arguing, which was threatening to disrupt my rediscovered focus. Ben followed me. You would think with all this supposed magic surrounding us— visiting the Magic Kingdom thirty times, being reminded constantly that we were in the most magical place on earth—we could all get along for one measly week. But no. There wasn't enough fairy dust in the world for that to happen.

As soon as we turned the corner, I stopped.

"That's it. We're doomed," I said.

Ben nodded.

Even he knew what this meant. There was yet another Kodak Picture Perfect Spot sign staring at us, instructing one and all to start clicking away. As if our mother needed any encouragement. We had not been able to pass a single one yet without her making us stop and pose. Now, I wouldn't have had a problem with these Picture Perfect signs if there had only been, say, one or two in the whole park. But they put one up every ten feet. How could that many things be perfect? Just because there was some cloudy lake we were all supposed to knock each other down to get the shot? Disney must have been so used to patronizing its visitors that they figured they might as well tell them where to point their cameras. I personally was sick of these photo shoots. My parents thought that having countless pictures with fake smiles would mean we were a happy family having a fabulous time, when in actuality we were all just miserable. It was obvious why they had dragged us here, and why every moment had to be catalogued even more so than usual. This was their last chance to get us all together before I left for college and couldn't be forced to do this kind of stuff anymore. The last hurrah. Before it was too late. Well, unfortunately it was too late.

And I knew if I was sick of these photo shoots, Ryan was borderline desperate.

"Everyone line up here," Mom said.

"Not any more pictures. We have enough to last until forever," Ryan said.

"Get in line," Dad said.

"I'll take it, then," Ryan said.

"No, I want all of us in this one," Mom said, looking around for a friendly chump to take it.

She walked up to a grown man wearing a Goofy hat. We had seen these ridiculous things all over the place. It consisted of two droopy ears, cartoonish eyes, and a pair of buck teeth on the edge of the brim. It was a pretty smart choice, if you asked me. If anyone was going to take your picture, it was a guy in a Goofy hat. And it didn't take a rocket scientist to predict if guys who wore Goofy hats were likely to be in great shape or sporting a pot belly.

"No, really, I'll take the picture. I don't need to be in any more," Ryan said.

Dad suddenly grabbed him and pulled him off to the side. It seemed like he was really clenching Ryan's arm. Frankly, I was shocked.

No matter how angry any of us kids had made him, he had never touched us like that.

"You should know by now that your mother likes to have her family's picture taken. If that's what she wants, then that's what you're going to do. I'm sorry that you have to go on all these rides and take all these pictures, Ryan. I'm sorry if it inconveniences you, but that's too bad. You need to learn to think of someone other than yourself for once in your life. Now, you're going to go over there, and you're going to smile for that camera, and you're not going to say a word. I don't care if she wants to take fifty pictures, you're just going to stand there and smile until your teeth ache. You got it?"

"Fine." Ryan ripped his arm out of Dad's grasp and marched over next to Ben and me.

"We're all miserable here," I said to him quietly.

"I don't want to talk about it," he said.

Then he turned toward the camera and grinned as if someone had just asked to see all of his teeth, fillings included.

"Say Disney World," Goofy Hat said.

"Cheese!" Ryan said really loudly. Dad said Disney World and nobody else said a word.

As soon as we got close to Spaceship Earth, Ryan charged toward a bench and sat down, crossing his arms and looking straight ahead. Mom told him to wait for us there, and then we headed toward the golf ball.

I just had a feeling.

Before we reached the entrance, I told Mom and Dad that I really needed to use the bathroom. Dad started to protest, so I said it was for girl reasons (one of the few perks of being the only female child was pulling out that card occasionally) and that I would just meet them at the exit when they were done. And it worked—Dad squirmed but did not argue. Instead I found a spot where I could see Ryan but was hidden from his view, and I watched. He was kicking his feet and sitting on his hands and scowling at the families walking by, but that was all. In other words, Ryan being Ryan. I contemplated going over there to try to talk to him, but what would I say this time that I hadn't already said a hundred different ways to him? And why would he suddenly listen now, with the mark where Dad grabbed him still fresh on his arm?

As I stood there watching this sullen kid, all I could think was, I can't save these people. And the next thought that seemed to flow logically from that one was, why should I have to? I had Disney fatigue, I had Sampson fatigue, and I had eldest child fatigue—I was tired of this phony place, of these annoying people, and of feeling responsible for others when no one had ever stepped in to help me with anything.

I decided I needed a walk alone, so I really did go to the bathroom. And when I came back, the bench was empty.

I looked in every direction, but there was no sign of him. I walked around the pathways near the bench, and then to the bathrooms and back, thinking he might have gone there. I figured there were three possibilities: he was hiding out in the bathroom, he had wandered off in defiance to buy some food or souvenirs, or he had run away. I didn't even consider abduction or anything along those lines—I was basically 100% certain that his anger was behind this. I looked over at the exit of Spaceship Earth, where they would be walking down the ramp soon. I thought of Ben in the car climbing that golf ball, staring right past the Pharaoh and Neil Armstrong, lost in his own world.

And then something in me let go. It was as if I had been gripping a kite in a storm and I finally let it slip from my hands. Almost like being in Ben's trance. As I looked at this empty bench where my angry brother had been sitting no more than ten minutes ago, I could already see my parents' reactions—the panicky father, the fragile mother. And I felt numb toward it all. Numb and detached.

I stayed near the exit. The bench was not in their line of sight, so I could have broken the news to them before they rounded the corner to see their missing son for themselves. But I didn't. What if I weren't here, I asked myself. The kite flew higher.

"Where's Ryan?" Mom said.

"What?" Dad said, somewhat startled.

"He's not on the bench," Mom said.

An elderly woman was sitting there now, while the rest of her family stood nearby, waiting as she took her break.

"OK, OK, that's definitely the bench he was on, right?" Dad said.

"Oh God. We have to tell someone here, or the police," Mom said.

"All right, maybe he's just in the bathroom," Dad said. "Let's all wait by the bench and I'll go check in there."

Then he looked at me, and it was as if he suddenly remembered that he had a daughter, or more specifically one who had been out here the whole time while they were in the golf ball.

"You didn't see him? When you went over to the bathrooms?"

"No, I didn't see him," I said

"I'm going to go look in there," Dad said.

Mom, Ben, and I stayed by the bench while Dad went to search. I was craning my neck and pacing around the bench to make it seem like I was searching in earnest for Ryan, but it was actually part of the trance: I didn't want to talk to Mom, or even see her reaction, and this playacting was a way to prevent that.

I saw Dad making his way back from the bathrooms, sans Ryan. I wondered what his next move was going to be, if he was going to keep looking on his own or decide to involve an outside party. Then, when Dad was about thirty feet away from us, a voice came over the loudspeaker.

"Would the Sampson family please report to Guest Relations?"

Dad stopped in midstride and stared at us, as if to say, that's us. They're talking about us. Then he hurried over to the bench.

"Where is Guest Relations?" Mom said.

Dad drew out his trusty map and steered us there. We didn't have to walk far, which was lucky for them—I could only imagine what my parents would have done if we had to take a boat or walk through 60 "countries" to get there. I looked over at Ben, who was trailing his frenzied parents. He just waltzed right into Guest Relations with his sly smile, as if this were hide and seek and we were all supposed to find Ryan. But I won the game and found him first. He was sitting on a chair against a wall, and he looked small and afraid.

As we approached Ryan, a security guard materialized and strode toward us with way more authority than he deserved in his Disney-issued uniform.

"What happened?" Dad said.

"I'm afraid your son did this." The guard held up a Kodak sign pointing the way to a camera shop. It was smaller than the Picture Perfect Spot signs, but they definitely looked related. Maybe first cousins. Somehow Ryan had managed to nearly separate it from its green pole, and it was now dangling toward the ground. It looked like an almost-decapitated, colorful flower.

"I'm sorry," Ryan said.

Dad stuttered a few times, like a toddler who was trying to remember the word for something but could only manage to get the beginning sound out, and then was quiet for a while.

"Of course we'll pay for the damage, sir," Dad said finally.

"I don't think there's any need for that. Just keep an eye on him for the rest of the day."

"Oh, we will, sir. No doubt about that."

Funny how Dad was acting like this guy was a military general or something. I was surprised he didn't salute him.

"Good to hear. Enjoy the rest of your stay in Disney World," General said.

"Thank you. And I apologize for my son's behavior," Dad said. He turned around and we all followed him out of Guest Relations like a flock of ducklings.

He stopped when we were outside.

"Ryan, I don't even know what to say. I can't believe you would do something like this."

"I'm sorry."

"Why did you do it?"

"I don't know."

I was wondering the same thing. What had he hoped to achieve by destroying the sign? Had he planned on taking it back with him to the bench so he could be holding his little trophy when we all returned? Or maybe he just wanted to throw it away so nobody could find the store and buy more cameras to take imperfect pictures at hackneyed spots.

What did he think, though? They had an army of sweepers following you around to collect your straw wrapper 0.7 seconds after you dropped it, so of course they were going to have an oversupply of security staff. Maybe the whole point was to get caught and keep the negative attention flowing. For all we knew, Ryan might have done it right in front of the General.

"Do you know what you put your mother through? She planned an entire vacation for you, and this is how you repay her. What did we just talk about half an hour ago? Did you think of anyone but yourself?" Dad said.

"I'm sorry."

"Come on, everyone. We're leaving," Dad said.

"For the day?" I said.

"What? Why are we leaving? It doesn't close for hours. We don't have to leave just because of this," Ryan said.

"Oh no, we're leaving," Dad said.

"Mom, we don't have to leave. I won't do anything else," Ryan said.

She didn't answer him.

On the walk to the tram, I remained in my trance. If Dad wanted to create more drama, it was no skin off my back. I could stay in the hotel room with my words and block it all out while he and Ryan continued their never-ending saga. Just keep me out of it.

I half-expected Ryan to bolt at any moment. But he didn't. He just kept his head down and was quiet on the tram ride.

"I'll drive," Mom said. She was probably scared Dad would crash the rental car in his mood.

We all climbed into the car, and Mom started driving out of the parking lot. Everyone was quiet.

"Ryan," Dad said. "I think you owe this family an apology."

"It's not my fault. I don't know why I did it, but I know it's not my fault. It's this family's. It makes me bad."

"That's ridiculous. What you did was incredibly embarrassing. Did you see how that man looked at us?" Dad said.

"What do you care what some security guy thinks?" Ryan said.

Then I turned around and looked at Ben, quarantined in the backseat. He was looking in Dad's direction, and for the first time during one of these fights I felt like he understood exactly what was going on.

It woke me from my trance.

"Look at us. Look at this so-called family. All we ever do is either completely ignore each other or fight," I said.

Dad seemed puzzled by this new entrant in the Dad/Ryan fight.

"That's not true," he said.

"Yes it is. We never have nice, normal conversations like other families. We keep all this crap in our house, a house that nobody ever visits. Ever. Look at our basement. Ten thousand scrapbooks. God knows how many dented cans. It's like a museum. We don't go anywhere except for Nonnie's and Disney World. We can't ask you about anything, especially anything about our own relatives. I don't even know how you two met. And Ben makes all those noises," I said.

"No, it's not—"

"Yes, Dad. All those things are true. And it's not normal. None of this is normal. We can't even have one good day here, in goddamn Disney World. We're the exact opposite of this place," I said.

"She's right. Why did we even come here? Disney can't fix this family," Ryan said.

Dad turned to Ryan, back in familiar territory.

"I'm sorry, that we aren't providing you with a vacation that meets your standards. I'm sorry it was such a disappointment that you felt the need to destroy someone else's property," he said.

"I didn't say that," Ryan said.

"This is the best your mother and I could do. If it isn't good—
"

"OK Dad, I get it," Ryan said.

"Well, I'm sorry. I'm sorry everyone hates this family and hates this vacation," Dad said.

"Stop saying you're sorry all the time!" Ryan said.

"I cannot wait to get out of here," I said quietly.

"I wish I could get out too. I'm so sick of this family," Ryan said.

"Me too," Ben said.

We all turned around and looked at him.

"See. Even Ben's unhappy. This can't be good for him. Nobody else sees what it's doing to him, but I do."

My eyes started to water. I pulled my lips tightly against my teeth to keep them from quivering.

"All right, that's enough," Dad said. It sounded more like a question than a statement.

"I'm going to run away," Ben said.

"Oh God," Mom said.

"Ben wants to run away?" I said. I had never once spoken to him about Huck and the raft. It had never even crossed my mind that the idea would appeal to him—leaving all of his comforts, his routines.

"Look at this. This family is a joke. Now even Ben wants out," Ryan said.

"We all want out," I said.

"I'm going to run away," Ben said.

None of us said anything. We just let that sentence hang in the air. Ben's voice sounded so soft and innocent compared to our harsh, emotional voices.

"There are things," Mom said. "Things you don't understand."

Dad turned his head toward her. "Sue."

"There are things. You don't, you can't understand. We tried our best," Mom said.

I couldn't see Dad's face. I could only see Mom's eyes in the rearview mirror.

"What are you talking about?" I said.

I watched her watch the road.

"Before Ryan was born, there was another . . .we had another child. A daughter. She died before her second birthday."

No one moved, not even Ben, for at least a minute.

"What did she die of?" Ryan said.

"Sparks," I said.

"I'm sorry, I just wondered," he said.

"She had a disease called Spinal Muscular Atrophy. It was diagnosed when she was five months old," Mom said.

"Is it like muscular dystrophy?" I said.

"Sort of." She paused, and I could hear her take a breath. "It's a disease of the spinal cord, and it affects your muscles. It makes them weak. Very, very weak. She had the worst kind possible, Type One. If you have that type, you don't live past two years old. She was never able to lift her head. When you held her, she felt floppy. It was like holding a rag doll. And she had trouble swallowing, so feeding her wasn't easy. Then it got worse."

"What happened?" Ryan said.

"She had to have a tube inserted into her stomach. She couldn't eat on her own anymore," Mom said.

"And she went on a ventilator. They gave us a portable one to use at home," Dad said.

I looked over at him. I had forgotten he was even there. This seemed like Mom's story, not his.

"Why didn't we get it?" I said.

"There was a twenty-five percent chance that any of our children would," Dad said.

The odds worked out perfectly, I thought.

"There was no cure?" Ryan said.

"There still isn't one," Mom said.

No cure. No hope. It was so final. How could they really

know? There was always someone who was told there was no hope the day before they found the cure. Always.

And it was a girl. That was the one thing I could always claim as my own in this family. But this meant I hadn't truly been able to all along. They had lived this secret, earlier life that had nothing to do with me. Or with Ryan or Ben.

"Wait a minute. That means Nonnie and Grandma Lyons— and the grandpas. They all must've known," I said.

Mom nodded.

"So all of our relatives know? And nobody ever told us?" Ryan said.

"You mean Aunt Lydia knows? That stupid—" I said.

"Hannah," Dad said.

"And she treats us like that?" I said.

"Seriously, is she human?" Ryan said.

"Wait, weren't there pictures? There has to be," I said.

"They're under the crawl space," Mom said.

I turned around. I realized he hadn't said anything the whole time.

"Hey. You all right?"

"Yeah." He was twirling He-Man's arm in little circles.

"You sure?"

He nodded.

"Oh God. We didn't ask what her name was," I said.

"Karin," Mom said.

"People in town must have known," Ryan said.

"Yeah, it must've been in the paper. How come no one ever accidentally told us?" I said.

"We moved," Dad said.

"We did? I thought you and Mom bought our house right after you were married," I said.

"We used to live in Fairtown. Before Hannah was born," Mom said.

"So you moved because of what happened?" I said.

Dad turned around and looked at us for a few seconds, and then faced forward again.

"The house we were living in was small, anyway. We decided we needed a bigger one," he said.

"How old would she have been?" I said.

"Twenty. Twenty on Monday," Mom said.

"What? Monday would have been her birthday?" Ryan said.

"Not would have been. It still is," I said.

"Is that why we came here in October?" Ryan said.

"No," Mom said.

"It's just a coincidence?" Ryan said.

Mom nodded.

"Where is she buried?" I said.

"All Saints Cemetery in New Prospect," Dad said.

That was when it struck me. If there was a cemetery, there was a grave. And if there was a grave, there was a body. A tiny body, forever under the ground that was my sister. Sister—that was another word that had only applied to me until now, and it was also something that I had always longed for. A confidant.

"I want to go to the cemetery," I said. "Was there a funeral?"

"Of course," Mom said.

"And everyone went? I can't believe none of our relatives accidentally told us. Steve must not know. He would've told us," I said.

"They didn't tell him," Mom said.

I looked into the rearview mirror. My poor mother. She looked so worn out. I couldn't imagine what she must have been through. All that sadness, and all in secret. Her eyes looked dead, and I just wanted to climb over the seat and hug her.

"You didn't want to tell us?" Ryan said.

They didn't answer him. We were all quiet for a little while.

"I'm so sorry," I said. I realized nobody had said that to them yet. Mom started crying a bit then, and she finally looked at me through the mirror.

She pulled the car over to the side of the road so she could switch seats with Dad.

Nine

December

Karin Elizabeth.

I would say the name to myself sometimes as I was going through my day, almost like a chant.

Karin Elizabeth. Karin Elizabeth.

It was as if someone had been shaking a can of soda for a long time and decided to open it that afternoon in Disney World. At first, as the soda gushed from the can, it seemed like it was never going to stop. But eventually the spray died down, and everything became still. And there was still a can of soda left to drink. It was just three-quarters full.

Things did change after that day, but not nearly as much as you might think. You just couldn't expect drastic changes from people— that was what I had decided. Maybe that was how it happened in the movies, neat and tidy, but in real life people just didn't change much, even if they probably should. Although I had to admit that I initially thought they would. Flying back home from Disney, I was positive that my family was forever changed. The clouds would part, the plane would land, and we would step into a new time, a new family. A magic portal. We, the people on that plane, would soon be able to look back at our old selves and think oh right, *those* people. I remember them. But that didn't happen. Definitely not with my parents. Dad still obsessed about germs, Mom still got her headaches. They were like two people who had been stuck walking the same dirt path for a long time, so long that the soles of their shoes had been worn down to practically nothing and the path had been carved so deeply they could not switch course.

The person who changed the most, really, was me. First off, I started talking to Mom about Karin. I waited a week before I really started asking a lot of questions, and she didn't deflect them like I thought she might. It was strange to finally talk to her in the way I always thought mothers and daughters were supposed to—sharing emotional stories, not shying away from weighty issues like grief and death. We had certainly moved beyond James Bond movies.

She told me about the time Karin got pneumonia. How she coughed up blood in the car. They had put a mat over the stain, but Mom always knew it was still there.

She told me how she would listen for an hour at a time to Karin's breath. She would put her ear to her sunken chest and just listen. Each breath was an effort, Mom said, something she had to try at every single time. No one could understand what it was like to have a baby who couldn't breathe.

We looked through the pictures together. Mom emerged from the basement holding a wooden box with a carving of a sparrow on its front. And here I had thought all along that there was nothing of value down there. Thought it was all junk. And out comes Mom cradling proof of my forgotten sister in her arms. She and I chose a picture to put out on the mantle. Nothing showy, just a small photo of her smiling at a balloon. She loved balloons—Dad told me that. He didn't talk much about her, though, and I didn't press him. As unfair to him as it may have been, I still saw this as Mom's story.

I wondered if they had lived in constant fear that we would find out accidently. It was certainly possible that we would, especially when you were relying on other human beings to keep your secret. Had they felt like they always had to tiptoe around us? And were they at all relieved to be free of that secret—relieved to know that at least their children had been able to hear it from their own parents? These were questions I would probably never feel comfortable asking them.

But the truth was they had been successful in keeping this

secret from us. For sixteen years. That was a little difficult for me to accept, because I had always seen myself as something of an expert on the Sampsons, and boy did this catch me by surprise. I had looked at my parents as a riddle I had solved long ago. Turns out that riddle was much more complex than I'd realized.

As for Ryan, he did calm down a bit, but only slightly. At least there probably wouldn't be any more Kodak sign maulings for a while. Honestly, he lost interest in the Karin story pretty quickly—he seemed satisfied just knowing the basic details. That was enough for him. You'd still most likely find him holding an electronic game instead of a history book. Again—you couldn't expect people to change much.

And Ben. I looked over at him. He was just sitting there calmly, holding his He-Man in his lap. His reaction definitely took me by surprise. When we all went to the cemetery, nobody said much except for him. It was probably the most he had ever spoken at one time. Is Karin (except he pronounced it Karen) in heaven? Is Grandpa Lyons with her? Do you think she can hear us? Will we ever get to see her? It was easy to underestimate him. He may have ignored Father's incoherent homilies or EPCOT's didactic rides, but when it came to the meaty stuff, Ben was taking in a lot more than we realized.

This was what I now understood. This was the Hannah Creed. 1) You were responsible for what happened to yourself, and 2) you had to take care of yourself first before you could help anyone else. Write that down on the tablets. The Two Rules. Life handed you what it handed you, and then you were in control from there. Crying about it didn't get you anything except a couple of bloodshot eyes and a runny nose. I had pretty much always understood rule 1. It was rule 2 that was my real discovery. After you realized 1, you needed to go back and help your family. But not until you had taken care of yourself first. Because otherwise you'd be in no shape to do it.

Proof of the creed:

After one of our longest conversations about Karin, when I was feeling closer to my mom than I probably ever had, I brought up the idea of having a professional evaluate Ben. She wasn't exactly chomping at the bit, but at least she didn't dismiss the suggestion outright. I planned on bringing it up again soon. I didn't want to overwhelm her, but I was pretty adamant about it. I think deep down she knew it was long overdue, and perhaps was even grateful that someone else was trying to take control of the situation.

And I started reading to him. We were already a few chapters into *Huck Finn*. I knew he didn't understand everything he was hearing, but I figured it couldn't hurt. And he did seem to genuinely look forward to our reading sessions.

Of course I was still planning on going away to college— possibly far away. But the difference was this: before Disney, I thought of that journey as an escape, pure and simple. Just like old Gatsby, don't look back. But now, I was tethered. I had Ben to think about. I couldn't just abandon him. I saw my car and my college education as part of a plan to better myself, while knowing I would always have to keep one eye focused back in North Prospect. But I knew that I had to leave—it was either me first and then Ben someday or neither of us at all if I stayed here. While I hadn't given up on Ryan completely, I only had so much to give, and Ben needed my focus now. He deserved it. He had been born into the family at a time when all of the various dysfunctions had really begun to take root, and I had to try to help cut him out of the jungle that had grown up around him.

Dad pulled into Nonnie's driveway, and then we all lined up to get something to bring inside. We had spent Thanksgiving with Grandma Lyons, so this was the first time we were seeing everyone on Dad's side since our trip. I was pretty sure they hadn't told anyone that we knew, and I could just imagine the nightmare scenario of Ben spilling the beans. Can we set a place for baby Karin? Can she have some apple juice? We'd all have to jump up and start performing the Heimlich maneuver on everyone as they choked on their Beanie Weanies.

I walked through the front door and handed Aunt Lydia the crock pot I was holding. Right away she gave my tomboy pants a snide look, so I knew that either they hadn't told her or if you cut her chest open you'd find a piece of coal there instead of a heart.

We went outside for a little while with Steve, and then Mom called us in for dinner. Before we sat down, Aunt Lydia said she was going to the front porch to get some more apple juice. I followed her. My heart was pounding very loudly, and I was annoyed at my body for having such a strong, uncontrollable reaction to a person I didn't even respect.

"Hi Aunt Lydia."

She let her eyes sort of roam around my face and then held them still. I suppose that meant go ahead, Inadequate Niece.

"I just wanted to let you know that my mom told us." I paused. "About our sister."

But there was no need to add the sister part. As soon as I said Mom told us, the muscles around her eyes began moving and twitching, as if she were trying to blink but was somehow being prevented from doing so. She did this a couple of times before finally blinking.

"She did?"

"Yes."

"She told all of you?"

I nodded.

"When?"

"Over two months ago." I counted backward to October in my head just to be sure. It seemed so much longer than that.

"Well, I'm sorry you had to hear it."

"I'm glad they told us."

She looked at me without saying anything.

"And Aunt Lydia. I'm sorry about Eddie." I turned around and went back to the table without seeing her reaction. Her reaction, to be honest, didn't matter to me.

I let out my breath. My legs were shaking and my heart was still obnoxiously loud, but I was relieved. I had done the thing I'd been rehearsing for weeks, because somehow I knew it would fall to me to tell her, and then she would pass the information along to everyone else when we weren't there. I was proud of myself for actually having gone through with it—I had not taken the easy way out and mumbled never mind when confronted with those cold eyes of hers. I liked to believe I was tough, but the truth was I had never really had a serious conversation with a single adult other than my parents. At least now I had proven to myself that I could do it.

#

Number one killer of children under two years old. I wondered if they knew that. The doctors might have told them, if only to let them know they weren't the only ones going through it.

Fifty percent chance of the sibling being a carrier of the SMA gene. Twenty-five percent chance of the sibling being completely normal. Well, I was pretty sure none of us Sampson kids could ever be considered normal, even if our genes happened to be. I hadn't told my parents that I had looked all of this up, not even during my conversations with Mom. I figured I would tell Ryan and Ben what I'd learned someday. There was no need to do it anytime soon.

Poor Mom. I don't think she ever let Karin go. She was just waiting in the basement the whole time. And together Mom and Dad had turned our house into a secret, constant wake, allowing only themselves to attend. And I was the fool who kept asking why nobody ever came over. I wouldn't have wanted anyone over, either. And I probably would have taken countless pictures of my children, too, and overprotected my youngest. Although the other day when I had suggested having Christmas at our house, they hadn't immediately say no. To even just consider the idea was a pretty big step for them.

The doctors must have told Mom that we could be carriers of the gene, but you could understand why she didn't want to tell us, even with those odds. She probably wanted us to go through life without ever having to worry about something so stark. But she couldn't hide the past from us forever. Or maybe we couldn't hide from it. I bet the past always finds everyone eventually. There's no home base.

I think they truly believed that they couldn't tell us. That if they did, we couldn't be a good family. A perfect family. We were their second chance, and they wanted to make sure they got it right this time around, and that meant shielding us from the gory details of the adult world. But having that secret there, lying underneath us, buried in the basement while we walked over it day after day, only made us worse. So I don't think this was the year it all went downhill. I think we were always down at the bottom. We didn't know any other way. And by Disney, we had somehow gotten even lower. Maybe we fell down a manhole or something. And in the car that afternoon Mom finally understood this and tried to fix it before it was too late. What I realized that day in English class was true: No family's perfect. I should get that made into a bumper sticker, slap it on my Civic. You never know, it might help someone in NO Prospect to see those words. The truth. There was no such thing as normal. Everyone had their problems, and thinking you could be perfect if you only tried hard enough wasn't just wrong or stupid. It was dangerous. It only made things worse.

The funny thing was, Dad almost got it, with his dented cans and duct-taped door handles. He understood that things could be a little damaged but still be useful, too. They still had value. Well, maybe not dented cans of creamed corn. That stuff was God awful. It had never had a drop of value and never would.

I elbowed Ben.

"Hey, want to play twenty questions?"

"Yeah."

"Hold on. I need to think of something hard since you're turning into such a pro," I said.

He inspected the back of his new He-Man while he waited for me. This one actually held real caps. When you pulled He-man's arm back and then released it, he would take a punch and the cap would explode. In about two hours, Ben had used up all the caps that had come with it. I almost fainted when he opened it this morning. It was by far the best and most dangerous present Dad had ever bought him.

"OK, I've got it."

"Is it Dad's purple crystal?"

I smiled. "No, that's one. Remember, you have to ask more general questions, like is it heavy, can you eat it, things like that. And I won't ever reuse the old ones, so don't guess them."

"Can you touch it?"

"Yes. Good question. Two."

"Is it round?"

"No. Three."

"Do we own one?" Ryan said. He was sitting in the third seat, playing the handheld game I had bought him for Christmas. That wasn't my only gift to him, though. I had also given him a laminated copy of my SAT prep notes.

"No. That's four."

"Is it in my room?" Ben said.

"If we don't own one, how can it be in your room?" I said.

"Oh yeah," Ben said. He made a bomb noise and dug He-Man into the gap between the seats.

"I won't count that question. You're still on four. Ask another one."

"Is it a person?" Ben said.

"Yes. Very good. Five."

"Is he related to us?" Ryan said.

"No. Six."

"Is he old?" Ben said.

"Be more specific. What do you mean by old?"

"Not a kid," Ben said.

"Yes, the person is an adult. That's seven. How do you both know that he's really a he?"

"Is he male?" Ryan said.

"Yes, eight."

"You made us waste a question," Ryan said. "Male, adult, not related to us."

"Did we ever meet him?" Ben said.

"Yes. Nine."

"Does he kill bugs?" Ben said.

I laughed. "Yes! Ten."

"Is it Anthony?" Ben said.

"Yes, it is. That's eleven. How did you know it was Anthony?"

"I knew."

"Eleven, that's the new record. Good job."

Ben smiled and went back to inspecting his He-Man.

I rested my head against the window. We passed by a small woods, no bigger than two of our backyards, and then the moon appeared out of nowhere. It was a crescent moon, very bright, but you could still make out the shape of the full moon behind it, like in eclipse pictures. It was how I'd always imagined the moon would look from the raft. A complete circle, dull and faded, with a beautiful little piece of it showing through.

Made in the USA
Lexington, KY
14 December 2012